LAURIE

NAME: Laurie Hunt

AGE: 14

NATIONALITY: British

STUDYING: Singing, drama

ROLE IN LUCKY SIX:
Lead singer and songwriter

PERSONALITY: Inquisitive

INSTANT-MESSAGE NAME: LuckyStar

JACK

NAME: Jack Hunt

AGE: 12

NATIONALITY: British

STUDYING: Music

ROLE IN LUCKY SIX:
Bass guitarist

PERSONALITY: Cheeky

INSTANT-MESSAGE NAME: CaptainJack

NAME: Aimi Akita

AGE: 13

NATIONALITY: Japanese

STUDYING: Music

ROLE IN LUCKY SIX:
Lead guitarist and wannabe singer/songwriter

PERSONALITY: Outspoken

INSTANT-MESSAGE NAME: RockChick

NAME: Marybeth Fellows

AGE: 13

NATIONALITY: American

STUDYING: Music, dance

ROLE IN LUCKY SIX:
Keyboard player

PERSONALITY: Caring

INSTANT-MESSAGE NAME: CurlyGirly

ELLE

NAME: Elle Beaumont

AGE: 14

NATIONALITY: French

STUDYING: Singing, dance

ROLE IN LUCKY SIX:
Band manager and backing singer

PERSONALITY: Very efficient!

INSTANT-MESSAGE NAME: ElleB

NOAH

NAME: Noah Hansen

AGE: 14

NATIONALITY: American

STUDYING: Music, drama

ROLE IN LUCKY SIX:
Drummer

PERSONALITY: Laid back

INSTANT-MESSAGE NAME: DrummerDude

NAME: Sasha Quinn-Jones
AGE: 13
NATIONALITY: British
STUDYING: Dance
PERSONALITY:
A snooty show-off who's got it in for Lucky Six

NAME: Chelsea Woods
AGE: 13
NATIONALITY: British
STUDYING: Dance
PERSONALITY:
Sasha's sidekick – with more talent in her little
finger than her friend has in her entire body . . .

Chapter One

It all started when Ms Lang announced that this year's summer show was going to be a serious spectacular. Big, sensational, epic – that sort of thing. Not that it's normally a snooze-fest or anything. It's just that this year is special. But I should probably go back a bit, right?

Ms Lang is our headmistress. The 'Verity Lang' part of 'The Verity Lang Academy for the Performing Arts'. That's our school and, as schools go, it's pretty cool. I mean, we still have to do normal stuff, like maths and geography, but somehow when double maths is sandwiched between modern dance and a drama rehearsal, it's way less boring. When Ms Lang first started the academy, it was just for dancers. Or 'hoofers', as my brother Jack so unhilariously puts it.

But then she decided to rope in some extra teachers and bingo – The Verity Lang School of Dance became The Verity Lang Academy for the Performing Arts. That was twenty years ago. Totally ancient history. But also the reason for this year's supersized summer spectacular. A twentieth anniversary showcase, our drama teacher, Mrs D'Silva, calls it, although it'll be way more exciting than that sounds. The academy's been buzzing ever since we found out. Practically the whole school auditioned, including me. I'm a singer in a band and the show's all we can think about just now. Which was why it was kind of amazing that I was the first person to see Mrs D'Silva's list.

I'd been to the dentist and, according to the clock over the main doors, it was ten minutes after the start of lunch break when I got back. The entrance hall was quiet and deserted, apart from a dark-haired figure wearing a long, floaty skirt and an armful of clanking bangles.

'Hi, Mrs D'Silva,' I said. She was pinning something to the noticeboard.

'Laurie!' she said, beaming. 'You're just in time. This is the summer showcase programme. Big excitement, eh?'

'Cool,' I said, feeling a familiar pang of nerves. Auditions aren't usually that big a deal around here. They happen about as often as science lessons. We're all just as used to rejection as we are to success, but when you're competing against each other, it's kind of different. More important somehow.

'Cheerio,' said Mrs D'Silva, smiling at me again and clanking back off towards the staffroom.

I took a deep breath, walked across the hall to read the list, and there we were.

Amphitheatre, 7.30 p.m.
LUCKY SIX
(Music) Laurie Hunt; Aimi Akita;
Marybeth Fellows; Noah Hansen; Elle Beaumont;
Jack Hunt

Last on the bill, playing the outdoor stage. Seriously awesome.

3

I glanced over the rest of the list to see who else had aced the auditions. There were thirty performances altogether, split between the amphitheatre – which Mrs D'Silva's husband was building out in the grounds – and the academy's indoor theatre, Fonteyn Hall. The programme was arranged in two columns, one for each stage. As I skimmed through the names on the second, I froze.

Fonteyn Hall, 7.20 p.m.
LAST ORDERS
(Comedy sketch) Dan Piper, Noah Hansen

Yep. That's the same Noah Hansen. Tall, curly hair, amazing blue eyes and a totally brilliant drummer. But definitely just the one of him, supposed to be on two different stages at practically the same time. I sighed, and made my way out into the grounds where I knew the others – along with most of the school – would be helping Mr D'Silva.

The amphitheatre was Ms Lang's idea. She said that as well as meaning we could invite more people to the show, it would give twice the number of students a chance to perform. Or, in Noah's case, the same number of students, twice as often. As I walked towards it, I spotted Elle and Aimi, sitting a short distance away. Not exactly a surprise – Elle hates anything involving dust, dirt, paint or sweating

and Aimi's a genius at worming out of hard work. I waved them over and carried on towards the half-built stage. Noah and Marybeth were busy painting a set of steps that led up to the raised stage, and I guessed Jack wouldn't be far away.

'Hey,' said Noah, looking up. He had a streak of black paint across one cheek and I could see two clumps in his hair, as well.

'Hi.' I grinned.

Did I mention I have a major crush on him?

'How was the dentist?' said Marybeth, but before I could answer Aimi and Elle arrived.

'Wow!' I said, staring at Aimi's head. 'When did you get that done?'

'D'you like it?' she said, pulling a freshly dyed strand of poker-straight blue hair forward. 'I thought streaks were more rock 'n' roll than just plain black.'

'Rock 'n' roll works for me, babe,' said my younger brother, Jack, jumping down off the stage next to us.

'Grow up, Wart-face,' I said. 'Like someone as gorgeous as Aimi would ever be interested in you.'

He stuck his tongue out and I shook my head.

When our last bass player left the band, it had taken the others nearly a month to convince me Jack should replace him. In the end, I had to admit he was surprisingly talented. When he painted 'Lucky Six rock!' across his puny chest in green paint and crashed the stage at one of our gigs, I finally realised how committed he was to the band and gave in. Doesn't stop him being annoying, but at least we sound good.

'What's up, dudes?' said Noah, dropping his brush back into the tin of black paint.

'Mrs D'Silva just posted the summer showcase programme,' I said.

They stared at me.

'And?' said Elle.

I grinned. 'We're on it.'

'No way!' said Aimi.

'You're kidding!' Noah gaped.

'Last act of the day, right out here on the amphitheatre stage,' I said.

We all went a bit wild then. Aimi squealing, Jack whooping, Marybeth jumping up and down and Elle smiling serenely.

'Whoa,' said Noah, sinking down on to the steps as he took the news in. 'Outdoors and at the end. It's like headlining a festival.'

'Your all-time favourite daydream,' I said.

'Totally.' He nodded.

'Noah,' said Elle.

'Yeah?'

8

'The steps,' she said.

He lifted up his hands, which were now completely black, then stood up and turned round. 'Paint still wet?'

'Oh, yeah,' said Jack.

'Unless you were wearing zebra-striped trousers before you sat down,' said Marybeth.

Noah slapped a hand to his forehead and that turned black too.

'Enough!' I giggled. 'Listen, there's something I forgot to tell you. Something Noah forgot to tell us, actually.'

He looked at me blankly.

'Auditioning twice for the same show?' I said.

'Oh,' he said. 'That. Yeah. But the band got through, and that's what counts.'

'Not just the band,' I said. 'Your comedy sketch with Dan's on the list too.'

'No way!' he said excitedly.

'You auditioned with us *and* with Dan?' said Elle.

'Yep.'

'Out of everyone who auditioned, and didn't get

9

through, you got picked twice?' said Aimi.

'What can I tell you?' Noah smirked. 'I'm incredibly talented.'

Marybeth punched his arm and Aimi kicked him in the shins.

'Hey!' he protested, rubbing his arm and spreading even more paint around.

'The point is,' I said, 'we're on at seven thirty out here; you and Dan are on at seven twenty inside. You can't do both.'

'It'll be fine,' he said. 'The comedy thing's ten minutes, tops. I'll come straight out here and we can just start a few minutes late.'

'That so won't work,' I argued.

'It will,' he said. 'No worries.'

Seriously. So chilled he's practically a one-boy ice-cream factory.

'What about clothes?' said Elle. 'What's your costume for the sketch like?'

Noah's face fell. 'Like someone who works in a burger bar,' he admitted.

'Perfect,' said Elle sarcastically.

10

'Please welcome onstage,' said Aimi, holding an invisible microphone, 'Lucky Six, featuring the amazing drumming talents of Billy McBurger-Boy!'

Jack made crowd-roaring noises and the rest of us laughed.

'So, what are we going to do?' I said, after a few minutes.

'Ask Mrs D'Silva to change the programme,' said Elle.

'Yeah, like that'll happen,' said Marybeth. 'Have you heard her going on about how difficult it was fitting everything in?'

'It can't hurt to ask,' I said.

'Sounds like you've just volunteered for the job,' said Aimi.

By the time everyone else had arrived in the common room after lessons, I was already waiting. Mrs D'Silva had let us out of drama early, and I had some lyrics to finish.

'So?' said Aimi, dropping down into the chair next to me.

I closed my battered lyrics book as the others sat down, then grinned. 'Sorted,' I said.

Jack whooped again, and Noah practically bounced off his seat.

'I still get to do both, right?' he said. 'Play with you guys *and* do the comedy sketch with Dan.' He glanced across the room at Dan – his best friend outside of the band – who gave him this kind of lame boy-salute thing he's always doing.

I nodded. 'We're still the grand finale, and she swapped you and Dan with another sketch earlier in the show.'

'Awesome,' said Noah. 'Thanks. You know, for sorting it. And sorry I didn't tell you guys about the whole two auditions thing,' he added.

'Forget about it,' said Aimi, stretching out so both legs dangled over the arm of her chair. 'If I'd listened to Mum and Dad, I'd have auditioned twice as well.'

'How come?' said Elle.

'They wanted me to try out for a violin solo, as

well as doing the band audition,' she said. 'Way too much hassle. I'll just tell them I was having a bad violin day.'

'Aren't they coming over for the show?' said Marybeth. Aimi's parents live in Japan, and she boards here with the rest of us.

'Yeah,' said Aimi. She pointed at her newly blue hair. 'I figured this will distract them from asking about anything else, though.'

Jack smirked. 'Are everyone's parents coming?' he said.

'Yep,' said Noah.

Elle and Aimi nodded.

'Not mine,' said Marybeth sadly.

'Sorry,' said a voice behind us, 'did you just say *Noah's* parents are coming to the showcase?'

Sasha Quinn-Jones. Year-nine prefect, talent-free zone, official troll.

'Yeah,' said Noah.

She giggled and twisted a strand of shiny blonde hair round one finger. 'Brilliant!' she simpered, looking straight at Noah. 'I've always wanted to meet your mum and dad. Hey, Chelsea,' she said, turning to her almost-as-annoying best friend. 'Did you hear? Greg Hansen and Michelle Albright are coming to our summer show.'

'Shut *up!*' squeaked Chelsea Woods. 'That's, like, incredible.'

'What's incredible?' said a boy with dark hair, sitting next to the window.

'Greg Hansen and Michelle Albright are coming to the showcase,' Chelsea told him. 'The movie stars,' she added, as two nearby girls looked up, impressed.

'Is that true, Hansen?' asked Rufus Donovan, the boys' year-eleven prefect. Like Marybeth, he was an American scholarship student. Unlike Marybeth, he was totally jealous of Noah and didn't usually bother talking to him unless he had to.

'Er, yeah,' said Noah. Half the common room seemed to be listening in on the conversation now, and he looked majorly uncomfortable. 'I, uh, need to talk to Dan,' he said, after an awkward pause. 'About our sketch.' He stood up and bolted across the room to his friend.

Sasha watched him go, looking annoyed.

'Come on,' she said to Chelsea. 'We've haven't got time to hang around talking to no-hopers.' And she stalked off, Chelsea scuttling behind her and Rufus Donovan following in their wake.

'She's right,' said Marybeth. 'Not about no-hopers,' she added, seeing Elle's indignant expression. 'About having other stuff to do. I've got a ton of homework.'

'Me too,' said Elle.

The two of them gathered their stuff together.

'Coming?' said Elle.

'In a bit,' said Aimi.

'I just want to finish this,' I said, picking up my lyrics book again.

Even though the way everyone had been talking about Noah's parents was pretty lame, I had to admit it would be kind of cool to meet them at last. I'd known Noah for two years, ever since he auditioned for the band. The fact his parents were movie stars was kind of well known around the school, but he never made a big deal of it, so none of us did either.

15

There was no escaping the fact, though – they were real-life, mega-successful actors. What Mrs D'Silva would call 'positive role models'. I bit the end of my pen, wondering what I'd find to talk to them about.

Questions for Noah's film-star parents
  1. How do you prepare for big movie roles?
  2. What's the best thing about making films?
  3. Do you help each other learn lines?
  4. What would your dream acting job be?
  5. What's it like to work with someone you're dating?

'Hey,' said Noah, leaning over the back of my chair. 'Where's everyone gone?'

I jumped and automatically snapped the book shut. How long had he been standing there and, way more importantly, had he seen what I was writing?

'Homework,' I managed to say, as he moved round to sit opposite me.

It could have been worse, I guess.

Final question

   6. Is your son cute, or what?

It's only a bit more obvious.

    Honestly? I may never need to wear blusher again.

Chapter Two

'What, in the name of frilly tutus,' I said, as Jack sat down at our lunch table the following day, 'is that?'

His plate was practically heaving under the weight of everything he'd stacked on it, and there was a reddish-brown pool forming on the tray underneath.

'Sausages, mash, roast chicken, roast potatoes, baked beans, two eggs, mushrooms, stuffing, brown sauce and gravy. Oh, and a carrot,' he said, holding it up. 'I'm on a bit of a health kick.'

The day the lunch hall went self-service was the happiest of my brother's sad little life. Elle looked a bit faint at the sight of so much random food. Enter Laurie Hunt, expert subject-changer.

18

'So, I booked a music room for our first show rehearsal,' I said, as Jack plunged a fork into the mountain on his plate. 'Tonight at five thirty. It's the one opposite the maths room.'

'Twelve c,' said Elle, probably the only student who knows all the room numbers in our warren of a school off by heart.

'OK with everyone?' I said.

'Sure,' said Noah.

'Five thirty,' Marybeth repeated.

'Mmm-mmmmm-mmm,' said Jack, through a mouthful of disgusting mush.

Aimi prodded her salad.

'What's up, Aims?' I said.

She wrinkled her nose. 'I talked to my parents.'

'Uh-oh,' said Noah.

'Tell me about it,' said Aimi. 'They're totally on to the whole not auditioning for a violin solo thing.' She stabbed at a tomato and it pinged across the table. 'It just really bugs me,' she continued, as Marybeth picked it up. 'I need to prove to them playing in the band isn't a waste of time. I mean, it's still music. I'm still good, right?'

'Course,' I said.

'It'll be cool,' said Noah. Pretty much his answer to everything.

'It's all right for you,' Aimi grouched. 'Your parents are way less uptight than mine.'

'Yeah, right!' he said. 'Like, they're not bugging me ten times a week about my grades and concentrating more in acting class. "There'll be plenty of time for bands and drums when you've finished studying",' he said, in an excellent imitation of his mum. 'At least they'll get to see me do both at the showcase,' he added.

'We have to be *so* good,' said Aimi fervently. 'The best Lucky Six gig ever.'

'For parents' sake.' Noah grinned.

'Not just parents,' said Elle. 'There'll be hundreds of people at the show. Who knows how many bookings we could get if they're impressed.'

Elle, in case I haven't mentioned it, is our manager and publicist as well as a brilliant back-up singer. Perfectionist, super-organised and, when it comes to landing us gigs, a total genius.

'Big bookings,' said Noah dreamily. 'Like festivals or concert halls.'

'Millionaire parties and celebrity weddings,' said Marybeth.

'Arenas and stadiums,' added Aimi.

'Pubs,' said Jack.

I love it when we get all ambitious like that. I know the others are hoping their parents will be impressed at the show, but for me – and Jack, as well – it'll be our older brother, Matt, whose opinion matters most. That stuff about festivals and arenas? It's not just a dream for him. His band, Hype, have a massive record deal and they're totally living it. If Matt thinks we're good, maybe we really do have a chance of making it big.

'Aimi's right,' I said, as Jack got stuck back into his gruesome lunch. 'We have to make this the best show we've ever done, starting tonight.'

Running 18. B there soon. ☺ N

'Noah's going to be late,' I told Aimi, Elle and Marybeth, reading his text. We were all standing, as planned, outside the music room.

'Surprise,' said Elle.

I grinned.

'Oi, girlies.'

Jack, strutting down the corridor. Our parents would be so proud.

'What's with the gossiping?' he said. 'Standing around like a bunch of old ladies when you could be inside setting up.'

He pushed heavily against the music-room door with one shoulder and yanked the handle down.

'Ow!' he yelped, rubbing his shoulder when the door didn't budge.

'Locked.' I smirked. 'That, Brainache, was what we were – did he say gossiping? –'

'Oh, yeah.' Marybeth nodded.

'– *gossiping* about.'

Jack scowled. 'What's happening, then?'

I checked the time.

'Mr Hooper said five thirty, and it's nearly twenty to six now.'

'Five thirty-eight, actually,' said Aimi, pressing a button on the super-techy new watch her parents had sent over the week before. They both work in what Aims calls 'gadgetry' in her home city, Tokyo – communications and electronics mostly – and her room is pretty much full of the amazing stuff they mail over to her. 'One thirty-eight p.m. in New York, three thirty-eight a.m. in Sydney,' she said. 'In other words, time we got started.'

'They don't normally lock rehearsal rooms until everyone's finished,' said Marybeth.

I looked back down the corridor for the hundredth time, hoping to see Mr Hooper – our music teacher – scurrying towards us, jangling his keys. Instead – Sasha Quinn-Jones. Just brilliant.

'Oh, look,' she said, sneering. 'Losers. I thought there was a weird smell down this corridor.'

'Get lost, Sasha,' I snapped.

'I wouldn't talk to a prefect like that if I were you, Hunt,' she said.

23

'"If I were you,"' sighed Aimi. 'Think of that, girls. If Sasha were a nice, normal, talented human being like Laurie.'

Elle and Marybeth giggled.

'Shouldn't you be upstairs doing your homework?' said Sasha quietly, staring straight at Marybeth. 'I heard they kick scholarship students out if their results slip.'

'Yeah, and I heard talentless halfwits can't get into the academy, no matter how rich their parents are,' I said. 'Guess it just proves you can't believe everything you hear.'

'Clever.' She smirked. 'But will it still be funny when you're in detention for hanging about in corridors after the end of lessons?'

'Er, hello?' said Jack. 'This is a music room. We've got a rehearsal here.'

'No,' said Sasha. 'This is a corridor. That –' she pointed at the door of 12c – 'is a music room. Do I see you inside?'

'It's locked. We can't get in,' said Jack, before I could do the world a favour and gag him.

24

Sasha's porcelain-perfect face cracked a smile.

'Locked?' she said. 'Genius. It's like someone knew you were meant to be practising and thought they'd save the rest of us a big fat earache.'

'Leave it,' said Elle, as I opened my mouth to argue back. 'We're meant to be rehearsing, remember? Not arguing with her.'

'I know, it's just –'

But Sasha seemed to have decided she'd won.

'Later, losers,' she said, stalking off down the corridor, and I realised Elle was right. Totally not worth it.

'Let's go find Mr Hooper,' suggested Marybeth.

'I really am dreadfully sorry,' said Mr Hooper, as we all stood outside the room again ten minutes later. 'I know I had them in the staff room earlier.'

'Can't be helped,' grunted Mr Brown, the academy caretaker. He was working his way through an enormous bunch of keys, trying to find the right one for 12c.

Mr Hooper frowned and dug about in the pockets of his geekalicious beige jacket again.

'Here we go,' said Mr Brown suddenly. He pulled a key from the bunch, turned it in the lock and stepped inside the room to flip the light switch on.

'Good job, Mr B,' said Jack, following him and dropping his bass down on to a desk.

'You're the best,' said Aimi, flashing her best grin.

'Not a problem, kiddos,' said Mr Brown, rubbing

26

his shiny bald head. 'Enjoy your rehearsal. I'll come and lock up again in an hour or so.'

Me, Elle and Marybeth followed the others inside and started setting up.

'Most grateful,' we heard Mr Hooper say as Mr Brown made his way back out into the corridor. 'I, er, don't suppose I can trouble you to, ah, furnish me with a replacement set of keys?'

'Well,' said Mr Brown, 'it's not really policy. Too many keys hanging about the place. It's a security risk, see.'

'Of course, of course,' said Mr Hooper.

'Leave it with me,' Mr Brown said, the two voices getting fainter now. 'I'll sort something out for you.'

'Dudes,' said a third voice. My stomach did a well-practised back-flip, and I turned round to see Noah pushing the door open. 'What have I missed?'

As it turned out, what Noah had missed wasn't even the worst bit of the rehearsal. We set everything up and got started pretty quickly, playing through our best stuff and agreeing what we should work on for the show. Then I sang the others this new song I'd been writing. I always get kind of nervous doing that, even though we've been together over two years now. But, if there's anyone I can rely on for an honest opinion, it's the five of them and, tonight, they loved it. Everyone, except Aimi.

'It's good,' she said, agreeing with the others. 'But something's missing.'

'Sounds perfect to me,' said Marybeth.

'We shouldn't mess with it,' said Noah.

'It needs . . .' said Aimi, thinking, '. . . a longer guitar solo.'

I love Aimi. Lead guitarist, kind of a diva, awesome onstage. But she has a thing about hogging the limelight. Like it's my fault I'm the singer.

Anyway, it all got messed up after that.

'The solo's exactly the right length,' I told her.

'It's way too short,' she argued, 'No one will even notice it.'

'Notice you, more like,' I mumbled.

'What, behind your big head?' she snapped.

'Like anyone wants to listen to a ten-minute guitar solo,' I said. 'Total dullsville!'

'Hey, maybe that's what we could call your song,' she said.

And that was when I stormed out. Rehearsal over.

It'll all be fine tomorrow. Me and Aimi argue all the time. We say stupid stuff, then apologise and everything gets back to normal.

The thing that was *really* bothering me once I got back to my dorm was how it had all gone so wrong. I'd been determined to have this perfect rehearsal. Brilliant first rehearsal = brilliant show, you know? And now I felt like everything was ruined. The locked door, Sasha, arguing with Aimi. Even my new song felt tainted and somehow spoiled by it all.

I dropped my stuff down on the bed and switched on my laptop. I honestly meant to get on with the enormous pile of homework that was threatening to topple off my desk, but, as the screen flickered to life, I sort of automatically hit the Internet and found myself staring at the home page of our web site.

Lucky Six, looking happy and confident and most definitely not arguing. I opened the gallery and scrolled through a pile of our performance photos. Most of them were taken by Miss Diamond, the academy's vocal coach, who usually chaperones our gigs. They were pretty good: Aimi and Jack doing their wild rockstar thing, Marybeth totally getting into it and Noah, gorgeous as you like. I smiled, feeling better. It was a bad rehearsal, not some stupid omen or jinx. As I went to log out, I noticed something flashing at the top of the message board.

New

I clicked on it and the message opened.

Lucky Six: SOS

Kind of weird, huh? I checked the sender name.

Guest

Totally helpful. Confused, I tapped in a response.

Who are you? What do you mean?

And then waited for a few minutes. I even opened my history book and thought about starting some homework. Every time I refreshed the page, though, the question was still the last thing there. No answer, or even any sign that Guest had read it. In the end,

31

I gave up. Maybe it was someone messing about. I switched the computer off, and decided to check back in the morning, just to make sure.

Chapter Three

Over the next few weeks, things were pretty crazy – rehearsing, revising for exams, the whole school getting ready for the showcase. But, for the six of us, our mystery guest's SOS message was distracting. I'd told the others the morning after I'd found it. We spent a while discussing whether it was just someone goofing around, and even talked about what SOS might mean.

'School Of Singers,' Elle had suggested.

'Maybe,' said Aimi, giving me a meaningful look, 'it's Short On Solos.'

I raised my eyebrows. 'Scared Of Songwriter?' I suggested, and Aimi grinned.

'Singers On Stilts,' said Noah, who can be really random sometimes.

'Seriously 'Orrible Songs,' said Jack. He shook his head. 'There's no pleasing some people.'

We all laughed. It wasn't till the following day, when Guest finally answered my question, that we started to take it more seriously.

Shock On Stage

Talk about disappointed. Like that explained anything. This time, it was Elle who replied.

What sort of shock? What's your name?

It took a while, just like the first one, but eventually a reply appeared.

Silence Or Sorry

'SOS again,' Marybeth said. 'I don't get it.'

None of us did. Every time someone posted a reply, the same thing happened. Waiting, then another SOS message.

34

'The thing is,' said Aimi, 'we don't know anything about him.'

'Or her,' said Elle.

'Exactly,' said Aimi. 'If he – or she – had a screen-name, even, it might give us a bit of a clue.'

The three of us were sitting in the music room again with Marybeth and Jack, waiting for Noah to arrive so we could start rehearsing. When Aimi had pulled out her laptop to check the web site, we'd found yet another SOS message:

Special Occasion Spoiled

And now we were playing our new favourite game, Guess Guest's Identity.

'Maybe they don't want us to figure out who they are,' said Marybeth.

'That makes it even fishier,' said Jack. 'I mean, if you're friendly, you don't go all mysterious and anonymous, do you?'

35

'You think it's an enemy, then?' I said.

'Does "special occasion spoiled" sound like good mates and a laugh a minute to you?' said Jack.

'I still think we should tell someone,' said Elle. 'Report it to Miss Diamond, or Mrs D'Silva.'

Elle's all about sticking to the rules and doing the right thing.

Aimi shook her head. 'They wouldn't be bothered. They'd just say it was someone's idea of a joke.'

'Which it probably is,' I agreed. 'A *bad* joke.'

'Hey,' said Marybeth, turning round as the door opened. It was Noah.

'Finally,' said Aimi, checking her watch.

I looked at Noah suspiciously.

'What's up?' I said. Being extra-sensitive to his moods is all part of my whole having-a-massive-crush-on-Noah thing.

He shrugged. 'It's nothing, really.'

The five of us stared at him expectantly.

'I lost a pair of sticks, is all,' he said. 'They went missing the day before yesterday, and I thought they'd have showed up by now.'

'They're probably in your room,' said Jack. 'You could lose a horse in that mess and it would be two weeks before you found it again.'

'That's the thing,' said Noah. 'I'm always losing stuff, but then it turns up again after a few hours.'

'Maybe they disappeared into the same weird black hole as Mr Hooper's keys,' suggested Marybeth.

'And Sasha Quinn-Jones's talent.' Aimi smirked.

'Is that where you've been?' Elle asked Noah. 'Looking for your drumsticks?'

He nodded. 'It's like they just vanished.'

'They weren't your lucky sticks, were they?' I asked.

'Uh-uh,' he said, pulling a set from his back pocket and waving them at us. 'That would've been a disaster.'

'So, you have sticks, there's no disaster and we're standing here talking about it. Why?' said Elle.

She had a point.

As we ran through the first couple of songs, I found myself getting more and more worried about how un-brilliant everything sounded. At this rate, we wouldn't even be ready for the showcase, let alone make it our best-ever performance.

'From the top,' I yelled, as the new song ground to a halt again. 'And, Aims, that's a major chord at the end of the chorus, not a minor.'

'That's what I played,' she snapped. 'Don't blame me if the song's not working.'

I opened my mouth to answer back, then changed my mind. Aimi was right. The new song wasn't working, and the old stuff didn't sound much better. We were already rehearsing three days a week after lessons and as often as we could at weekends, but it wasn't enough. I fidgeted anxiously with my microphone as we started the song again. With everyone revising for exams, and Noah rehearsing his comedy sketch too, was there any way I could convince them we needed more rehearsals?

It took a couple of days, but I finally decided it was our only option if we were going to be good enough for the show. I was on my way to talk to the others, when I ran into Marybeth.

'Hey,' she said. We were in the corridor outside the first-floor girls' dorms and it was the first time I'd seen her since lunchtime that day.

'What happened?' I said, gaping at the crisp, white sling on her left arm.

She frowned. 'I fell over in modern dance this afternoon. Mr Martinez was teaching us this new routine and I just slipped.'

'Are you OK?' I asked. I know – stupidest question in the world. OK does not wear a sling. 'I mean, how bad is it?'

'Sprained,' she said. 'The nurse checked it out and

put this on for me.' She pulled gloomily at a corner of the sling. 'I've got to rest, but she said it'll be OK in a few weeks.'

I bit my lip, holding back the question I really wanted to ask. It was way more important to make sure Marybeth was OK.

'I bet those new cleaners over-polished the floor,' I said, trying to sound cheerful. 'Aimi reckons they scrubbed the banisters in the main hall so hard she could see her reflection in them. It took me and Elle ages to drag her away.'

Marybeth smiled, but her eyes looked suspiciously watery. 'Tell that to Sasha. She thinks my cheap jazz shoes were to blame.'

'Cheap jazz shoes' is *so* Sasha. Her whole deal with me and Marybeth and the others? Totally because Marybeth is here on a scholarship. To any normal person, the fact Marybeth was talented enough to be picked from hundreds of students to win the scholarship is way more important than whether her parents could afford to send her here. But to Sasha, and her tag-along friend, Chelsea, the

41

affording bit is all that counts. Their problem with the rest of us, is that we're friends with Marybeth. Seriously shallow, huh?

'What would Sasha know?' I said, as Marybeth wiped her eyes.

'It wouldn't have been so bad if it had been the other wrist,' said Marybeth. I could tell she was trying to cheer herself up. 'At least then I might have got out of doing exams.'

'I don't s'pose they said anything about . . . you know, when you'll be able to play again? Keyboards, I mean. The band, and everything.'

Yep, that tactful.

'The nurse said a week or two before I can play properly,' said Marybeth. 'I asked straight away. I can still play with my right hand, though.'

She waved it about, as I tried to ignore the panicky feeling in my stomach. One more hiccup and we may as well say goodbye to our chances of being anything more than fingers-in-your-ears terrible at the showcase.

I smiled feebly. 'You'll still come to rehearsals,

though, right?' I said. 'One hand's better than nothing, and at least it'll mean you know what's going on.'

'Sure,' she said. 'I know it's only two weeks till the show, but we'll be OK.'

'Marybeth!' cried a voice from along the corridor. 'How's the arm?'

It was Sasha, walking towards us with an unconvincingly sympathetic look on her face.

Marybeth stiffened. 'Fine,' she said.

'Shame, isn't it?' said Sasha to me. She nodded at Marybeth's sling. 'Still, you could always take advantage and change your name to Unlucky Six. It's got kind of a ring to it.'

She smirked. I scowled.

'You know,' I said, suddenly realising something, 'it's kind of a coincidence that every time something unlucky happens, the one person we can count on to be hanging around is you.'

She raised her eyebrows so high they disappeared under her sharp fringe. 'For once, you've got it dead right, Hunt,' she sneered. 'Coincidence is *exactly* what it is.'

I stared at her, looking for any sign she might be lying, or I might be on to something.

Not a flicker.

'Anyway,' she sniffed, 'I've got way better things to do with my time than waste it hanging around *Unlucky* Six.'

'Like what?' I said to Marybeth, as Sasha stalked off. 'Polishing her broomstick?'

Marybeth giggled and, behind us, a door opened.

'I thought it was you,' said Elle, sticking her head out. 'Come and see what we've found.'

Curious, I followed Marybeth into Elle's room, and found Aimi sitting inside.

'I thought we weren't allowed to keep pets,' said Marybeth, and Aimi threw a cushion at her.

Elle ignored them, and pointed at her computer. 'There.'

'New message?' I said, staring at the web page on the screen.

She nodded, and scrolled down.

'Strike Off Sasha,' I read, amazed. 'How did they know?'

'Know what?' said Elle.

'That two minutes ago we were talking to Sasha in the corridor and I suddenly had this idea she might be behind the messages.'

'You don't think she could've realised what you were thinking, rushed back to her room and posted this message to put you off the trail?' said Aimi.

I frowned, thinking. 'I don't know. I don't think she'd have had time.'

'She definitely wouldn't,' said Elle. 'The message was posted at five oh seven. Ten minutes ago.'

We were all quiet for a minute, and I knew the others were thinking as hard as I was, trying to work out what it meant.

'What if,' said Marybeth eventually, 'the person who's leaving the messages hasn't been threatening us, but they've been trying to warn us about something?'

'Maybe,' I said. 'It does kind of make sense. Like, if they knew we were suspicious of Sasha, they might be trying to stop us wasting our time checking up on her.'

45

'What about the other messages?' said Aimi.

We scrolled back through the message board, reading them.

'Shock on Stage, Silence Or Sorry, Special Occasion Spoiled – they *could* all be warnings,' agreed Elle.

'Look!' said Marybeth suddenly.

The 'new' icon had popped up at the top of the page again, and we scrambled to open the message.

Search Out Secret

'I don't know about you three,' said Aimi, 'but I'd say there's some Seriously Odd Stuff going on.'

Chapter Four

OK, I have a confession to make. I am tidy. Not super-freak neat, just tidier than your average teenager. I've tried being messy, really I have, but it's not for me. This is how I see it in girl-maths:

Being messy + having lots of stuff ÷ living in a pretty small dorm room = boring time spent looking for things

Being tidy + knowing where everything is ÷ living in a pretty small dorm room = valuable time spent boy-dreaming (like daydreaming, but with added Noah-ness)

Clever stuff, no?

Which is why I was so surprised when my lyrics

book went missing. It might be old and battered, but it's way up on my list of Important Stuff I Take with Me Everywhere. Mobile phone, cherry lip balm, lyrics book.

Ideas can pop into your head at the weirdest times and, the night before, I'd been revising for our science exam with Elle, when I worked out how to fix the new song. All the words and music were in my book, and the minute I got back to my room, I'd scribbled the idea down.

'I'm *sure* I put it in my bag this morning,' I told Elle, who was helping me search. 'I remember thinking I'd sneak into the music room at lunchtime to see how the new bit in the chorus sounded.'

'The last time you saw it was lunchtime, then?' said Elle, lifting up my pillows to make sure the book wasn't underneath.

I shook my head. 'I didn't go in the end. Noah and Dan asked me to watch them rehearsing their sketch to check whether it's funny enough.'

'Is it?' said Elle.

I tipped my school bag out on the bed and started

double-checking the books again. 'It's really good,' I said, 'but the best bit was when Sasha walked past and saw me hanging out with Noah.'

If I haven't mentioned it before, Sasha totally has a thing for Noah. It might be the only thing we've ever agreed on.

Elle grinned. 'The blue-eyed monster,' she said.

'*Green*-eyed,' I giggled.

Even though her dad is English, Elle grew up in France with her mum. Her English is pretty much perfect but sometimes she says things that are just a bit wrong.

'I don't get it,' I said, stuffing the last book back into my bag. Still no sign of the one we were actually looking for. 'I never leave it lying around. How can I have lost it?'

'Come on,' said Elle. She'd been kneeling down, peering under the bed, but now she stood up and straightened her skirt.

'Where?' I asked, as she walked across the room and opened the door.

'We're going to retrace your steps,' she said.

'Wherever you went today, we go there again. I don't think the book's in here.'

'Me neither,' I admitted.

The retracing-my-steps thing seemed like a good plan and, seeing as it was the only one we had, I followed Elle out into the corridor.

'OK,' she said. 'You came out of your room before morning lessons, and then where did you go?'

'To the music studio,' I replied. 'Double lesson.'

'That's where we're going, then,' said Elle, and we headed downstairs, towards the main building.

'Have you checked the web site today?' asked Elle, as we walked.

'No,' I said. 'But I did kind of have another idea. About SOS, I mean.'

'OK,' said Elle.

I rubbed my nose absent-mindedly. 'You know last week when we were trying to work out whether the messages were a warning or a threat?'

'Yes.'

'Well, what if they're both?'

Elle paused. 'How d'you mean?' she said.

'What if the person leaving the messages is trying to warn us about someone else?'

She frowned. 'There are two people?'

I nodded. 'The person who wants to wreck our show, and Guest, who's been trying to warn us about it.'

'Why would anyone want to do that?' said Elle.

'I don't know,' I admitted. 'Not yet. But don't you think it's even a bit suspicious-sounding?'

'Not really,' said Elle. 'Overactive imagination-sounding, maybe.'

'Nice,' I said, faking a huff.

'That's what you get for being a drama queen with police officers for parents.' She grinned. 'It's a dangerous combination.'

She looped her arm through mine, still smiling, and dragged me into the music studio.

'Think about it,' she continued. 'Everything that's happened – Marybeth's accident, Noah's drumsticks, getting locked out of the music room – it's just coincidence. Stuff that could happen to anyone.'

'But the messages,' I argued.

'Crazy fan,' she said. 'Someone messing around. We're not being sabotaged, and you,' she added, elbowing me in the ribs, 'are not living in some cheesy soap opera.'

'OK,' I said, half an hour later when we'd finished retracing my entire day. 'I give up. My lyrics book is officially and totally lost.'

The two of us had gone back to the common room to grab a drink, and I was slouched on a squashy sofa.

'Hey!' I said, sitting up suddenly and spilling juice on my skirt. 'You don't think one of the others might have borrowed it to check some lyrics or something?'

'Not without asking you first,' said Elle, shaking her head at the mess I'd made. She pulled me over to the sink in the corner of the room and grabbed some kitchen towel.

'I s'pose you're right,' I said, still thinking, as she dabbed at the spreading juice stain. She handed me the kitchen towel and pulled some more from the roll. I opened the bin to throw it away and froze. There, on top of the screwed-up crisp bags and soggy teabags, was my lyrics book.

We stood and stared for a second, then I rolled up my sleeve and fished the book out of the bin. Elle took a few steps backwards.

'It's wet!' I said, dropping it down on the draining board. '*Soaking* wet.'

My stomach lurched as I opened it. No lyrics, no songs, meant no summer showcase. But it was OK. I turned the first few pages, flipped to the middle, then right to the back, and everything was still there. Soaking wet, but nothing Aimi's mega-powerful hairdryer couldn't sort out.

'Thank goodness for biro,' I said, my voice shaking with relief. 'If I used a fountain pen I'd have lost everything.' I peered back under the sink, hoping there might be a clue left in the bin. 'I just don't understand how it got in there.'

'Maybe you left it on a table and someone thought it was rubbish,' Elle shrugged.

53

I shook my head. 'I haven't been in here since yesterday afternoon. How could I have left it in here *and* written out those changes to the new song last night? It's impossible.'

'It doesn't make sense,' Elle agreed. 'Unless . . . I suppose someone could've taken it out of your bag.'

'I've had it with me all day,' I said. 'Even in the ballet studio, it was on the floor near the barre. Mrs Walsh would've noticed if someone had come in.'

'What about the canteen?' said Elle. 'It was so crowded in there at lunchtime; you wouldn't need to leave your bag lying around for a thief to grab something out of it.'

It was a horrible thought, even if it did seem like the obvious answer. Elle was quiet, and I was pretty sure I knew what she was thinking. If the book had been stolen, all of a sudden the idea of someone trying to sabotage us looked a lot less far-fetched.

SOS. Emergency mtg. Trunk room.
10 mins. B there! L x

I scrolled through my contacts and sent the text to Noah, Aimi, Marybeth and Jack, before Elle and I headed down to the basement.

'Why the trunk room?' said Elle, looking disgruntled.

'Because we all need to be in on this,' I said. 'The boys too, which means dorms are out.'

Boys in the girls' dorms, girls in the boys' dorms is strictly forbidden.

'And we need somewhere no one can overhear us,' I continued, 'which counts out the common room. This was the best place I could think of.'

I pushed the door open, and turned the light on. The trunk room is the place where all the boarders' trunks are kept during term-time. It's pretty dusty, which is why Elle doesn't like coming down here. Before it was a school, the main academy building was a hospital. It's huge and warren-like, kind of higgledy-piggeldy, I guess, and the trunk room is right at the bottom in the oldest part.

'Dudes,' said Noah, poking his head round the

door a few minutes after we'd arrived. 'Am I the first one here?'

'Yes,' said Elle. 'Me and Laurie are figments of your imagination.'

'That's meant to be funny, right?' he said, and I giggled.

Aimi and Marybeth arrived together a minute later, followed by Jack, who'd brought his bass.

'It's not a rehearsal, Brain-dead,' I told him.

'What've you dragged us down here for, then?' said Jack, annoyed. 'I was watching *Worst Ever Real-life Cop Chases Two* on that new satellite channel.'

'Quality TV,' nodded Aimi.

'Something's happened,' I told them. 'Me and Elle think it might be connected to the SOS messages and all the other stuff that's been going on.'

Even Jack stopped grouching then and, with some random chipping in by Elle, I launched into the story.

'Blimey,' said Jack, when I'd finished.

'Me too,' said Noah, who still hasn't worked out what 'blimey' means, even though he's lived in

57

England for nearly three years.

'It makes sense,' said Marybeth. 'Your idea about the messages being a warning, I mean.'

'And the fact someone might be trying to sabotage us,' agreed Aimi.

'My bet's still on Sasha,' said Jack.

'We already know it can't be her,' protested Elle.

'Even Guest thinks so,' said Noah. '"Strike Off Sasha", remember?'

'That doesn't prove anything,' said Jack. 'Just because Laurie and Marybeth were talking to her when that message was posted doesn't mean she's not behind the whole thing. She could've got Chelsea to do it for her.'

'She does do most of Sasha's dirty work,' said Marybeth.

'It can't be Chelsea,' I said. 'She's a day student. She wasn't there, so she couldn't have known we were getting suspicious of Sasha.'

'Well, I've heard this rumour,' said Jack, lowering his voice in a confidential kind of way, 'that day students have computers too. They can even access the Internet when they're not at school.'

'Ha, ha,' I snapped.

'And,' he said, ignoring me, 'boarders can do this amazing thing. I think it's called "phoning" the day students. Some of them have these gadgets so they can talk to day students, even when it's not day time.'

'OK, OK, we get your point,' said Elle.

'I *suppose* there's a chance it could've been Chelsea,' I admitted.

'Which means Sasha could still be behind the whole thing,' said Jack triumphantly. 'It all fits together. The way she keeps crowing over every little thing that goes wrong for us *and*,' he said, pulling a crumpled piece of paper out of his pocket, 'her dance thingy with Rufus at the summer show is on the indoor stage at the same time as we're performing outdoors.'

He handed me the paper programme for the summer show.

'Mrs D'Silva got them delivered today,' he said.

And there was Sasha's name.

Fonteyn Hall, 7.30 p.m.

Fire Duet

(Dance) Sasha Quinn-Jones, Rufus Donovan

'You reckon she's worried we'll steal her glory, or something?' said Aimi.

'Exactly,' said Jack.

'It does make sense,' I said, looking round at the others.

They nodded and yeah-ed.

I so hate it when Jack's right.

'Sasha's all about showing off,' I said, 'and we already know there'll be plenty of important people at the show.'

'The richer they are, the more desperate she'll be to impress them,' agreed Marybeth.

'It would be exactly like her to try and ruin things for us, just to grab more attention for herself,' said Aimi.

I rubbed my nose. 'She's not doing a bad job of it really, is she?'

Chapter
Five

'What we need,' said Elle, 'is a plan. A way to find out for definite if Sasha's behind it all.'

'Operation Sort Out Sasha,' said Noah. 'SOS.'

'Genius,' I said, and he flashed a smile back at me.

I drifted off for a bit after that. Pink cheeks, dreamy expression, that kind of thing.

'It's not bad,' Aimi was saying when I snapped back into reality, 'but how about we get hold of her costume for the show instead, and unpick all the stitching so it falls apart the minute she puts it on!'

'I don't think –' began Elle.

Aimi held up a hand to stop her. 'Getting into Sasha's room won't be any trouble. If you create a distraction, I can sneak in, no problem.'

'We can't do it,' I said.

'Why not?' Aimi demanded. 'She stole your notebook and Noah's sticks. And, if it weren't for her, Marybeth wouldn't be wearing that sling. It's revenge.'

'We don't know for definite it's her,' I said. 'That's the whole point of the operation.'

Aimi folded her arms, and leaned back against the wall, sulking.

'How come you get to make all the decisions around here?' she pouted.

'She doesn't,' said Elle. 'You're just being a brat.'

Aimi poked her tongue out, and carried on sulking.

'OK,' I said, ignoring her. 'How does this sound? Tomorrow lunchtime, a couple of us grab seats in the canteen as near to Sasha as we can, then start talking about how we're going to rehearse after lessons. If we talk just loud enough, she's bound to start listening in.'

'She *is* a champion earwigger,' said Jack.

'Exactly,' I said. 'All we need to do is drop enough

hints about where we'll be and when. If she follows us there and tries to mess things up, we'll know for sure she's the person trying to sabotage us.'

'I still think my idea was better,' said Aimi, kicking her foot against the edge of a trunk.

'I don't get it,' said Noah. 'Surely we'll just have wasted another rehearsal if Sasha messes it up?'

Elle gave him a withering sort of look.

'We lie,' I explained. 'Lay a false trail, you know? We'll say the rehearsal's going to be in one room but, really, it'll be somewhere else.'

'OK,' said Noah slowly.

'And, then,' I carried on, knowing what his next question was going to be, 'we set up a secret camera in the fake rehearsal room, so if Sasha does appear we catch her red-handed. Aims?' I added. 'Can we use that camera your mum and dad sent you last week?'

She stopped kicking the trunk, which was a good sign. 'Sure.'

'That's it, then,' I said. 'Operation Sort Out Sasha is a go.'

'You've thought of everything,' said Noah, sounding impressed. 'Pretty sneaky.'

I blushed and beamed, secretly pleased with my genius plan.

The others decided it should be me and Marybeth who staged the phoney conversation at lunchtime the following day.

'After the other night, she's got it in for you two more than the rest of us,' said Elle tactfully.

'She can't stand you,' added Aimi, not at all tactfully.

Marybeth shrugged. 'May just as well take advantage of it, I suppose.'

So, at the end of morning lessons, the two of us dashed off to the canteen to make sure we got seats as near to Sasha as possible.

'Over there,' I said, catching sight of her on the other side of the room with Rufus and Chelsea.

'Brilliant,' said Marybeth. 'There's a free table right behind her.'

We practically ran across the canteen, and grabbed the seats before anyone could beat us to it.

'Wow!' I said, dropping my tray on to the table. 'I'm starving.'

'Me too,' said Marybeth, copying my louder-than-usual voice. 'We'll be late for dinner this evening as well, what with the rehearsal and everything.'

I could hear Sasha behind me talking to Rufus about their duet. Good, because if we could hear her, she could hear us. Not so good, because if she was talking, she obviously wasn't listening.

'Oh, yeah,' I said, upping the loudness a notch. 'I'd forgotten about that. What time is it again?'

'Five o'clock,' said Marybeth. 'In the big music room.'

'Six b?' I said.

'That's the one,' nodded Marybeth.

There was a scuffling noise behind me, and I turned round just in time to see Sasha rolling her eyes at Chelsea and Rufus.

'We're going,' she told them, scooping up her half-finished plate of food.

Rufus looked like he might be about to protest.

'Why?' said Chelsea.

'You can't hear yourself think over other people's conversations in here,' she said. 'Why Unlucky Six think anyone's interested in their stupid rehearsals beats me,' she added, raising her voice so Marybeth and I couldn't fail to hear.

Chelsea sniggered, and Rufus stood up reluctantly. As they walked away, Marybeth breathed a sigh of relief.

'Mission accomplished,' I whispered, and she grinned.

The next stage of the plan was down to Jack and Aimi. They'd volunteered to set up the secret camera in the music room after lessons, then meet the rest of us back down in the trunk room.

Marybeth and I were sitting on piles of trunks, waiting, while Noah added the details of our summer showcase performance to the Lucky Six web site with Elle hovering behind him.

'I can't believe I forgot to do this,' she said. 'We should have put it on the news page weeks ago.'

'Take a chill pill,' said Noah, tapping away on his laptop. 'It's not like anyone can come to the show if they haven't got an invite anyway, is it?'

'Not the point,' said Elle.

'There might be some music big-wig, or talent scout who sees it and phones the school to get an invite,' I told him, repeating what Elle had said when I asked her the same question earlier on.

Noah finished typing and leaned back as the info automatically uploaded to the site.

'Thank goodness,' said Elle, relieved.

'Hey,' said Noah. 'New message on the board.'

By now, none of us was surprised when the word 'Guest' popped up, followed by the latest SOS.

Spy On Senior

'Chelsea, you think?' said Marybeth.

'Or Sasha.' I nodded. 'And totally fishy that it's

posted right before the time they know our rehearsal's meant to start.'

'*Fake* rehearsal,' said Noah.

'They're obviously trying to put us off the scent,' said Elle wisely.

'Shh,' said Marybeth, sitting up very straight.

There was a clanking outside in the corridor.

'It's the old service lift,' I whispered. 'Mr Brown uses it to bring the trunks up and down.'

'Not until the end of term, though,' hissed Marybeth.

As we listened, the lift thudded to a halt and the old wooden doors creaked open. Footsteps, and then voices. Two of them.

'It's Jack and Aimi,' said Noah, and the room relaxed again.

'How did it go?' said Elle, when they walked in a minute later. 'Is everything set up?'

'Yep,' said Aimi. 'No way anyone would know it's there. Jack found this box . . .'

'The one Mrs D'Silva's programmes came in,' Jack interrupted.

'We cut a tiny hole in it,' Aimi continued. 'Just big enough for the camera lens to see through, and I stuck it up on one of the shelves with a bunch of other stuff, pointing towards the door.'

'You did remember to press "record", didn't you?' I asked.

'How stupid do you think we are?' said Jack scathingly.

'Don't answer.' Elle grinned at me.

Chapter Six

If the others thought my plan to trap Sasha was good, it was nothing compared to their reaction when I revealed what I'd swung for our rehearsal that evening.

'Onstage, in the amphitheatre,' I told them excitedly. Exactly the same stage we were due to perform on two days from now. Totally cool, and totally what we needed.

'How?' said Noah. 'No one else is doing that.'

'Maybe they haven't asked,' I said. 'I went to see Miss Diamond; she checked it was OK with Ms Lang, and it was.'

'You know,' said Elle, once we'd all got over the excitement a bit, 'we should make it a dress rehearsal.'

'Yeah,' agreed Marybeth. 'That way we can check how the costumes look, and work out if we need to make any alterations before the show.'

'Just in case Jack has another trouser-splitting incident.' I smirked.

'*One* time that happened,' he moaned. 'It's not my fault they were badly made.'

'Hey,' said Elle.

'I'm just saying,' Jack told her. 'The proof is in my split trousers.'

'Proof of your giant bum,' I muttered.

Elle and Marybeth laughed. The two of them are our unofficial costume department. Marybeth, who's an amazing artist, does the designing, then Elle helps with the making. Mostly, it's just basic stuff like customised T-shirts or cool accessories, but for big shows like this one they spend ages making sure we look extra professional, costume-wise.

Once we knew our Sasha-trap was set in the music room, we all headed back to our dorms to get changed, and then out to the amphitheatre to start rehearsing.

'Your arm!' I said to Marybeth, suddenly noticing she wasn't wearing the sling.

'I know.' She beamed. 'The nurse said I was OK to start playing again. I've still got to wear this,' she added, pushing back the punky wrist-cuff she was wearing to show me a bandage underneath, 'but who cares as long as you can't see it.'

'It's so nice not to be worrying about what might go wrong,' said Elle, as we walked out on to the stage.

'I can't wait to go back inside and see what's on the tape,' said Aimi.

'We know what'll be on it,' said Jack. 'Sasha, caught red-handed.'

'Ready?' I asked, trying to stay focused as I adjusted my microphone stand.

We launched into the first song, which sounded way better than it had at any of our other rehearsals, then went straight into the new song. We'd tried it with the changes a couple of times already, but suddenly, out here onstage, it really worked. Just like I'd heard it in my head as I was writing it.

'Yeah!' shouted Aimi, as the last chord faded.

I turned round and we were all beaming, happy that things were finally coming together. Elle had jumped down into the audience area halfway through to check how the costumes looked. She pulled herself back up now, and we crowded round as she played back the video clip she'd taken with her phone.

'I took some photos too,' she said. 'We can print them out later, but it all looks good to me.'

'Cool,' I said. 'Let's run through everything one more time, then we'll go and check the tape.'

The second run-through was kind of rushed. We were all way more confident about the show now, and suddenly the idea of finding out what – or who – the secret camera had captured was the most important thing. We packed everything up as soon as we'd finished playing and, still in our stage costumes, made for the music room.

'Where's the light switch?' whispered Aimi, pushing the door open and fumbling about on the wall.

'There,' said Jack, stretching past her and flipping it on. 'Why are you whispering?'

'I don't know,' whispered Aimi, and Marybeth giggled nervously.

We all pushed in through the door, and Noah shut it behind us. In the few seconds it took for my eyes to adjust to the light and take in the room around us, Aimi and Jack had made their way over to a messy shelf next to the teacher's desk.

'No,' moaned Jack, burying his face in his hands. The programme box with its cut-out hole had been pushed to one side and Aimi's camera was lying uncovered on the shelf. Its tiny lens was pointing uselessly up at the ceiling, and there was a definite 'I told you so' kind of look spreading across Aimi's face.

'It was a good plan,' she said, as the rest of us moved closer to survey the scene. 'Shame it didn't work.'

I reached out and picked up the camera.

'We couldn't have known it would backfire,' Aimi continued, sounding smug. 'But it's not too late to try something else.'

'Like what?' asked Elle, as I pressed the 'playback' button and adjusted the camera's screen.

'My idea,' said Aimi. 'You know, taking the scissors to Sasha's outfit. We could call it Operation Slash On Sight. Or maybe Snip Off Sequins. Hello?' she added, realising no one was listening. Instead, they were standing around me, peering in at the little screen.

'What is it?' said Aimi.

'*Not* the ceiling,' said Jack. 'Whoever came in must've knocked the camera over afterwards.'

'Nearly five o'clock,' whispered Marybeth, pointing at the numbers in the corner of the screen. 'That was the time we said the fake rehearsal was due to start.'

'Look!' squealed Elle, grabbing my arm.

A figure had appeared behind the frosted glass in the door.

Jack dug an elbow in my back as he tried to get a better look at the screen and Aimi shoved Noah out of the way.

'Ow!' we both said at the same time.

'Is it Sasha? Is she coming in?' said Jack.

I stretched my arms out, holding the camera further away so everyone could see it without getting bruised.

'I hate to tell you this, Wart-face,' I said, 'but I think your Sasha theory's out the window.'

'No way is that her,' said Marybeth sounding disappointed.

Even through the glass you could tell the figure

was taller than Sasha with short, dark hair. Pretty much the opposite of her long, ice-blonde style.

'Maybe –' began Jack, who I knew wouldn't be happy to back down without an argument.

'Shh!' Elle interrupted.

The figure had just opened the door of the room, when someone else, shorter and with fair, curly hair appeared.

'Hello there,' we heard a voice on the tape say. I fiddled with the volume switch, turning it up as far as it would go. 'I didn't know you had keys to the music room.'

'It's Miss Diamond,' whispered Noah.

'Yeah, uh, Mr Hooper asked me to lock up,' said a male voice, pulling the door shut again. It was harder to hear after that, but we definitely caught the words 'Lucky Six', 'cancelled rehearsal' and 'favour'.

'He's pretending to be going out, not coming in,' hissed Marybeth.

The door opened again. 'Not to worry,' we heard Miss Diamond say. 'Just tell Mr Hooper you had to leave the room open for me. I've got a class first thing tomorrow, and I need to get things ready. I'll ask Mr Brown to lock up when I'm done.'

The male figure moved away and Miss Diamond came into the room, humming. She dropped a pile of books down on to her desk and grabbed two music stands.

'That's it!' said Jack, as the world seemed to turn upside down on the little screen. 'That's how the box got knocked off. Miss Diamond caught it with one of those music stands.'

We carried on watching, kind of nervous in case Miss Diamond spotted the uncovered camera. But then, I supposed, if she had, she wouldn't have left it on the shelf. The film was all ceiling now, but we could still hear what was going on. Clattering music stands, rearranging chairs, Miss Diamond humming and talking to herself. Then the door clicked open, closed again and we heard footsteps fading away along the corridor.

'Fast forward,' said Noah, after a few minutes' silence.

I whizzed through the rest of the film, eventually

hearing Aimi's voice ask where the light switch was.

'That's us coming in,' said Jack.

'Duh,' I said, as the screen went black and turned itself off.

'So, who was it d'you think?' asked Aimi, sitting cross-legged on one of the desks.

'He was pretty tall,' said Noah.

'And definitely someone who takes classes with Miss Diamond, because she knew him,' added Elle.

'But who do we know, apart from Sasha, who'd want to sabotage us?' I said.

'Maybe,' said Aimi, 'some boy has fallen desperately in love with me. You know, just from seeing me perform onstage, and now he's stalking me.'

'Yeah, that'll be it,' said Marybeth, trying not to laugh.

'I still think there was something –'

But before I could finish my sentence, a voice from the doorway made all six of us jump in horror.

'What the blazes do you lot think you're doing in here?'

Chapter Seven

S till frozen to the spot in panic, I heard someone start to laugh.

'Mr Brown!' I said, recognising the caretaker's familiar chuckle. I was so relieved my legs felt shaky.

'Yeah, that's me,' he said, rearranging his face as we all turned round. He was trying very hard to look stern. 'Should've known it was you lot. The famous Lucky Six. What do you think you're doing here, eh?'

'We, er, needed to, um . . .' I said, then trailed away, all out of excuses.

'Huh,' he grunted. 'Like that, is it? You know it's past seven o'clock, I suppose? You should all be in your dorms by now.'

'We were just on our way,' said Elle.

'Well, what are you waiting for?' he said, switching the light off.

We all scrambled down from the desks and pushed our way over to the door in the near-darkness as he shook his head and tried not to look amused.

'Chop-chop,' he said. 'I haven't got all evening. My dinner'll be in the dog if I'm not home soon.'

He held the door open as we filed out past him into the corridor.

'Enjoy your dinner,' said Noah, grinning, and we headed off as Mr Brown locked the door.

'What now?' said Jack, walking backwards a little way ahead of the rest of us. 'We can't just go up to our dorms and forget about it. We still don't know who that was on the tape.'

Aimi checked her watch. 'The common room'll be closing any minute,' she said, 'and I bet the corridor lights in the basement are already off, so the trunk room's no good.'

Honestly. You'd think we were living in the Dark Ages.

'Instant messaging,' I said. 'Everyone go back upstairs, and log on.'

'Always the boss,' said Aimi.

I pretended not to hear.

'Don't forget to take your costumes off as soon as you get back,' Marybeth called after Jack and Noah, as they walked off towards the boys' dorm wing.

'And hang them up,' added Elle.

What planet is she living on?

CaptainJack: Hurry up, girlies. You don't need make-up for online chats. That goes for you too, Noah.

DrummerDude: As if.

LuckyStar: Shut it, Wart-face. Our dorms are further away than yours. All here now?

CurlyGirly: Yep.

ElleB: Oui.

RockChick: What have I told you about talking French? If I can do the English thing, so can you.

LuckyStar: Hello? I thought we were meant to be talking about the tape. What have we got so far?

CurlyGirly: The person who tried to get into the music room is male and tall with dark hair.

RockChick: That rules out everyone in our dorm, then. ☺

ElleB: We know he's got Mr Hooper's keys too.

CaptainJack: So, either Mr H lost them, and Mystery Boy got lucky and found them, or he stole them.

LuckyStar: He's probably a boarder.

DrummerDude: How d'you figure that?

LuckyStar: Think about it. Mr Hooper is one of the staff wardens for the boys' dorms, so it would be much easier for a boarder to sneak into his room and steal the keys.

CurlyGirly: Even if he just found them, being a boarder doubles his chances. Mr H could have dropped them in the main building, or the dorms. Day pupils hardly ever go in the dorms.

CaptainJack: I reckon he stole them. It doesn't look like Noah's drumsticks got lost, does it?

LuckyStar: My notebook definitely didn't.

ElleB: Were the sticks in your room when they went missing, N?

DrummerDude: Yeah.

LuckyStar: Which proves the thing about him being a boarder again. It would've been way harder for a day pupil to get into Noah's room and steal them.

RockChick: If he's tall, it probably means he's older too.

CaptainJack: Or a freakishly tall year seven.

LuckyStar: Hang on. What was that message we got just before the rehearsal?

RockChick: What message?

DrummerDude: Another SOS.

ElleB: It was posted when you and Aimi were setting up the camera.

CurlyGirly: Spy On Senior.

CaptainJack: You reckon that means it's a senior who's behind everything?

DrummerDude: That would explain the tallness.

LuckyStar: Maybe Marybeth was right all along – Guest has been trying to warn us.

I leaned back from my desk for a minute as the others carried on messaging. Why had I listened to Jack's stupid theory about Sasha and Chelsea? We'd been much closer to the answer before, I was sure of it now. Jack had just been wasting everyone's time. I frowned. Not much chance we were going to find out anything else tonight, and I had an essay to finish for Mrs D'Silva before I went to bed.

LuckyStar: OK. So, the person we're looking for is a boy, tall, dark hair, probably a boarder and a senior. He's definitely got Mr Hooper's keys, and probably Noah's drumsticks too.

ElleB: And he has to have a motive for trying to sabotage us.

CaptainJack: He might not have it in for all of us. Or this could just be about us performing in the summer showcase.

My brain whirred. Something was falling into place. After the Sasha/Chelsea thing, I wasn't about to pay attention to another of Jack's ideas, but there was something in that last bit.

'Us performing in the summer showcase.'

And a motive for sabotage.

I dug around in my school bag, trying to find the showcase programme Jack had given me the day before. I pulled it out, and found what I was looking for.

LuckyStar: Brainwave alert. You don't think it could be Rufus?

DrummerDude: Rufus Donovan?

RockChick: How many other Rufuses do we know?

ElleB: Why him?

CurlyGirly: Of course! He's performing with Sasha at the show. They're doing a duet.

LuckyStar: Yep. Which means his motive is more or less the same as hers.

CaptainJack: What, he hates us and he wants everyone to be looking at his new frock instead of watching us perform outdoors?

LuckyStar: No. But their performance still clashes with ours, and he's always been jealous of Noah.

RockChick: That's true. Remember when he called you a show-off last term and said he'd report you if you didn't stop bragging about your – what was it?

CurlyGirly: 'Star-studded background.'

DrummerDude: Yeah. And all I'd said was I was going home to spend the holidays in New York. Like it's a crime to live there, or something.

LuckyStar: Remember how his ears pricked up the other week in the common room when Sasha was mouthing off about your mum and dad coming to the summer show?

ElleB: He was totally excited about meeting them. Maybe he wants them to watch his performance, instead of Noah's.

CaptainJack: That voice on the film could have been Rufus's too. I know it was muffled, but it did sound a bit like an American accent.

DrummerDude: This is heavy.

CurlyGirly: We don't know anything for sure, yet. It's just guessing.

LuckyStar: Deducing, not guessing.

ElleB: You know how we can find out for sure, though?

LuckyStar: Yep. Ask Miss Diamond.

DrummerDude: Smart.

RockChick: How did we not think of that before? Just ask her who it was she was talking to.

LuckyStar: Elle and I are in her vocal class first thing tomorrow. I can hang around afterwards and ask her.

CurlyGirly: Cool beans. Meet you at break to find out what she says?

ElleB: In the trunk room.

LuckyStar: It's a date.

CaptainJack: Does that mean I have to wash my neck?

RockChick: Shut up. You'll give me nightmares.

DrummerDude: Later, dudes.

Before I switched the computer off, I clicked on to the Lucky Six web site. No new messages. The last one was still 'Spy On Senior'. I signed in and tapped out a reply.

Rufus: Source Of Sabotage?

I lay awake in bed for a long time after that. The blue power light on my mobile flashed rhythmically on and off next to me, and I wondered about calling my parents. Professional police advice sounded like a pretty good idea right now. I knew they'd only worry, though. It's a parent thing. We'd come this far on our own, surely we could manage to fit the last bits of the mystery into place without anyone else's help. Except Miss Diamond's, of course. One question tomorrow morning, and we'd know for sure whether Rufus was behind the sabotage, or if we needed to start looking somewhere else.

Chapter Eight

For breakfast the next morning, I had three jelly babies, half a can of flat cola and a banana with more bruises than Jack got the time he tried stage-diving and the audience couldn't be bothered to catch him. Not because I'm a sugar fiend, like Noah, but because I slept through the breakfast bell and didn't wake up until Elle banged on my door fifteen minutes before our music class started. Mr Martinez and Mrs Walsh, who both teach dance, have this thing about how important it is to eat before the start of morning lessons. They practically make you swear an oath when you start at the academy saying you'll never skip breakfast. After a while, it turns into a habit, even if it does mean foraging for scraps in your dorm room when you oversleep.

Tired wasn't the half of it. Even when I'd managed to fall asleep, my dreams were full of shadowy figures, just out of sight behind doors, or disappearing round corners. After a night of wondering about the mystery messages and feeling guilty over the reply I'd posted without telling the others, my brain felt like cotton wool. The second I opened my mouth to start singing in Miss Diamond's vocal-training class, it was howlingly obvious my voice wasn't in a much better state.

'Concentrate, please, Laurie,' shouted Miss Diamond over the sound of our scale-singing. 'Remember, breathe and relax your jaw. Nice oval-shaped mouths.'

I tried. Honestly, I did. But my voice just wasn't working. My stomach lurched horribly as I remembered the show tomorrow and imagined not being able to sing properly then. But I knew it was just tiredness. Every time Miss Diamond told us to open our mouths wider, mine stretched into a yawn.

'Very nice, Laurie,' she said as I did it for about the sixth time. She obviously hadn't noticed my screwed-up nose and watery eyes.

Elle, who totally *had* realised it was a yawn, shot me a concerned look.

When it came to singing solo, though, there was no way anyone was being fooled.

'Did someone let a cat in here?' said Sasha, looking round the room after I'd croaked my off-tune way through a verse and a chorus.

'Maybe it fell off your broomstick,' I said under my breath, and got one of her famous death-stares in return.

Luckily, Miss Diamond moved on to Elle next and by the time everyone had sung their solo, the lesson was due to end.

'Laurie,' called Miss Diamond over the noise of scraping chairs as we gathered up our things, ready to leave. 'Can I see you for a minute, please?'

'I'll catch up with you,' I told Elle.

'Don't forget to ask about Rufus,' she said, lowering her voice.

I perched on the edge of a desk, clutching my books in front of me and tapping one foot nervously

against the chair in front. Now I was sitting in front of her, I felt kind of strange about telling Miss Diamond the whole story. Like saying it out loud to a teacher would make it seem less important, like silly schoolkid stuff. I suddenly realised that none of us had given a thought to what we'd do once we found the culprit.

'So, what's up?' said Miss Diamond, slipping some sheet music into a folder and coming over to sit opposite me. She's pretty sharp about spotting when stuff's going on with her students.

I hesitated, not sure where to start.

'Is there something outside of lessons that might be affecting your school work?' she said, trying again. 'I don't want to pry, but that was hardly your best performance today, and it's not like you.'

'It's the show,' I said. 'Tomorrow, I mean. The showcase. Well, not that exactly. Us. Lucky Six.'

Just *blabbering*. I took a deep breath and tried again.

'We've been having . . . problems. Not with each other,' I said, seeing her worried expression. 'It's someone else. We think they might be trying to sabotage our performance at the show tomorrow.'

'Go on,' she said, still looking concerned.

I told her about our first rehearsal and Mr Hooper losing his keys, then about Noah's drumsticks going missing, Marybeth's accident, my stolen notebook and the messages on our web site. I stopped short at the bit about the camera and the figure we'd seen on the film. It suddenly made everything sound kind of far-fetched, and I didn't think Miss Diamond would approve of us planting a spy camera in her classroom.

'We've been so determined to make it a brilliant performance,' I explained. 'Aimi's worried her parents don't want her to be in the band, and Noah's mum and dad aren't sure about it either.'

I trailed off, not knowing what else to say. I was sort of expecting Miss Diamond to come up with some brilliant idea to help us solve the problem. Even by academy standards, she's the coolest, almost not like a teacher at all. When she chaperones our gigs, we totally have a laugh with her and she really gets how important the band is to all of us. So, I was kind of surprised by the way she reacted.

'I don't know why you didn't come and talk to me sooner,' she said. 'Or one of the other teachers if you didn't feel you could come to me.'

'We didn't –'

'What were you thinking, trying to deal with it all yourselves?' she went on. 'Those messages should have been checked out by a member of staff right at the start.'

See what I mean? We needed help finding out who was behind the whole mess, not a telling off. But, before she could say anything else, the door opened and Mr Hooper's head peered inside.

'Sorry to interrupt, Miss Diamond,' he said. 'Have you got a copy of tomorrow's song list for the choir?'

'What?' said Miss Diamond, turning round. 'Oh, yes. For the show. Hang on.'

She fished around in the piles of paper on her desk and pulled out a neatly typed list.

'There you go,' she said, handing it to Mr Hooper, who looked stressed and relieved at the same time.

98

'Most grateful,' he said, before disappearing back out into the corridor.

The interruption seemed to make Miss Diamond lose her train of thought. Although, considering it was a fast train to Nothingsville, I wasn't too bothered.

'Right,' she said, glancing at her watch. 'I suppose I'd better let you go and get ready for your next lesson.'

I slid off the desk and picked up my bag.

'No more worrying,' she added. 'Everything'll be fine. You get up there tomorrow and knock them out, Noah and Aimi's parents included.'

I opened my mouth to argue. When was anything ever OK, just because someone said it would be? But I had a feeling it wouldn't make any difference.

'"Knock them out,"' I muttered, shutting the music-room door behind me. *We'd* be the ones getting knocked out at this rate. I mean, who was to say how desperate the culprit was? For all Miss Diamond knew, he could be plotting something spectacularly evil. I sighed. If we were going to stand any chance of solving the case, it looked like the six of us were on our own again.

It was too late to meet the others in the trunk room after that. I quickly tapped out a text, asking the five of them to meet me in the library at lunchtime, before dashing off to Mrs D'Silva's drama class.

'Why here?' hissed Aimi, as we walked past Mrs Gregory, the librarian. 'It's not exactly conversation central.'

'We want to know what happened,' whispered Jack. 'Why didn't you turn up at break?'

Without answering, I led them over to a row of computers below the library's tall, old-fashioned windows and pulled a chair up to the very last monitor, which was tucked behind the corner of a bookshelf.

'I need to show you something,' I whispered, as they dragged more chairs up to sit next to me. I tapped our web site address into the computer and waited for the site to load.

'What did Miss Diamond say?' Jack asked again. 'Was it Rufus outside the music room?'

'I don't know,' I admitted, and filled them in on everything Miss Diamond had – and hadn't – said.

'We don't know anything new, then,' Elle frowned.

'Well, we might,' I said, feeling kind of uncomfortable. 'I did something . . . I know I shouldn't have without asking everyone first, but it was kind of an impulse thing.'

'What?' whispered Noah.

'Last night,' I said, 'after we'd all been talking, I left a message on the board.'

I clicked on it and sat back for a few seconds to let them read it.

'"Source Of Sabotage?",' said Marybeth.

'You put Rufus's name on it?' hissed Noah incredulously. 'Wild.'

'What's the reply say?' asked Jack.

I stared at the screen, noticing the tiny 'new' icon

for the first time. I'd been so wound up about confessing, it hadn't even occurred to me the mystery guest might have replied. Impatient, Jack leaned across me and clicked the message open himself.

'Whoa,' said Noah, as we all read it.

Sleuths On Scent – signed, Sister Of Suspect

Chapter Nine

'You're not kidding "Whoa",' said Marybeth.

'I can't believe we were right,' I said faintly.

'*You* were right,' Noah corrected me. 'It was your idea, remember.'

I was too busy blushing to answer.

'This sleuthing stuff rocks when you get it right,' said Jack.

'So, what now?' asked Elle. 'Now we know for certain it's Rufus, I mean.'

'Shh!' hissed Mrs Gregory, appearing from behind the bookshelf.

'Come on,' I said, grabbing my bag as she bustled away. 'Let's find somewhere else.'

We left the library, Noah winking at Mrs Gregory on the way out and the rest of us trying very hard not to laugh at the appalled expression on her face.

'Too hilarious,' said Aimi, sinking down on to the grass when we got outside.

'This'll do,' I said, looking around. It seemed like a pretty quiet spot.

We all sat down, except Elle who reached into her bag and pulled out a neatly folded square of material. She spread it out on the grass, then gingerly sat on top of it, tucking her skirt underneath her at the same time.

'Comfortable?' grinned Aimi, who was sprawled out, leaning back on her elbows, picking at random bits of grass.

'Yes, thanks,' said Elle.

'Careful you don't get grass stains on that,' said Jack, nodding at the square of material.

Elle ignored him.

'You know,' I said, 'the more I think about it, the more I can't believe we didn't work all this out before. We wasted so much time on that whole Sasha idea,' I added, glaring at Jack. 'Of *course* it couldn't have been a girl.'

'Noah's drumsticks?' said Marybeth.

'And Mr Hooper's keys,' I nodded. 'A girl couldn't have stolen them. It would be easier to break into . . .'

'The safe where my mom keeps her favourite shoes?' suggested Noah.

'Exactly,' I said.

'It might've helped if the person leaving the messages had mentioned that bit about "Sister Of Suspect" before,' said Aimi. 'We know Sasha's an only child.'

'Hang on,' I said. I'd almost forgotten the 'sister' part of the message. 'Rufus does have a sister, doesn't he? I mean, does anyone know for definite?'

'Yep,' said Jack. 'They're twins. She lives back at home in America with their parents. I overheard him talking about it in the common room once.'

'And?' I said.

'And . . . then I went upstairs to play on this brilliant new computer game I'd just got. It was that one with the earth v aliens football match,' he said, looking at Noah.

'Cool,' said Noah. 'No way is that fair if you're playing on the earth team, though. The players on the other team have all got, like, three extra feet to kick with.'

I stared at them until they stopped talking.

'I *meant*,' I said, 'what was Rufus saying about his sister?'

'No idea,' shrugged Jack.

'He can't have just said, "I've got a sister", then started talking about the weather or the TV or something,' I said. 'Try and remember.'

He did. It looked quite painful.

'He was going on about them having an argument, I think,' said Jack slowly. 'Something to do with him not understanding what it was like to put up with their mum and dad all the time. He was telling that year-eleven girl with the wonky nose.'

'They don't get on, then?' said Marybeth.

Jack sat up, obviously remembering more of the conversation. 'That was what Nosy said, but Rufus told her it was a love/hate thing. Arguing one minute, close as you like the next.'

'Interesting,' said Elle.

'You think it's her who's been leaving the messages all along?' Marybeth asked.

'Of course!' I said, working out another bit of the puzzle. 'It makes sense. If she's in America, that's why it always took ages for the messages to get through. The time difference must have meant we were asking questions when it was the middle of the night over there, and she was posting replies when we were all asleep here. It totally ties up!'

'Yeah,' said Noah thoughtfully. 'And I heard

Rufus, a few weeks ago. He was on the payphone downstairs in our dorm-block. I didn't really pay attention at the time, but he was having a row. Shouting and yelling at someone on the other end of the phone.'

'Maybe he was telling his sister about sabotaging us,' said Jack. 'And if she was trying to talk him out of it . . . That could've been what they were arguing about.'

'We need a plan,' I said, thinking hard.

They all stared at me in silence.

'Hello?' I said. 'Just because we know Rufus is behind everything, doesn't mean he's not still trying to ruin the show tomorrow. "Shock On Stage", remember? He might be plotting all kinds of gruesome stuff.'

'Laurie's right,' said Elle. 'We need to work something out, or the show could end up being a disaster.'

'Just like my parents are expecting,' grouched Aimi.

'Mine too,' said Noah.

And I had a brainwave.

'Your parents,' I said to Noah. 'They're the reason Rufus is doing all this, right?'

'I guess,' he said, sounding somewhere between guilty and embarrassed.

'What if he found out they weren't coming to the show?'

'But they are,' said Noah. 'Their plane lands this afternoon. They've booked their favourite hotel suite and everything.'

'Rufus doesn't know that,' I said.

'Which means we could make him *think* they aren't coming,' said Marybeth, realising what I was getting at.

'The only trouble is,' I said, 'we've already staged one conversation for him to overhear, even though we thought it was Sasha who was listening in then. He'll never fall for the same trick twice.'

'Especially after he turned up in the music room and we weren't there,' Aimi pointed out.

'I could do it,' said Jack. 'I've got this camera rigged up to the door of my room so I can see when anyone's hanging about outside.'

'What do you need –'

'Don't argue with genius,' he said, holding up a hand to stop me talking. 'Rufus's room is along the same corridor as mine. Me and Noah could wait inside, leave the door open just enough for Rufus to hear through and as soon as we see him walking past . . .'

'. . . start talking,' I said.

'A bunch of stuff about how bummed Noah is because his parents aren't coming to the show after all.' Jack nodded. 'I bet Rufus won't even know it's my room. He thinks year sevens are well below him.'

'D'you think Rufus will buy it?' I said, looking round at the others.

'*I'd* believe it,' said Noah glumly. 'It wouldn't be the first time my mum and dad have bailed on me at the last minute.'

'I don't see why not,' said Elle.

Aimi and Marybeth nodded in agreement.

'This is going to be seriously cool,' said Jack smugly.

110

I'd been logged in to my instant messaging account
since we got back from dinner, but there was still no
word from Jack and Noah. Elle, Aimi and Marybeth
were hanging out in my room and, to pass the time,
we were looking through some of the photos on our
web site.

'Where's that one of Noah wearing his blue top
and looking all intense?' I said, as Aimi scrolled
through the pages.

'That one?' she said, clicking on a thumbnail.
Noah's picture filled the screen and I smiled
dreamily.

'Seriously gorgeous,' I sighed.

'He looks more constipated than intense, if you
ask me,' said Aimi. 'I just don't get what you see in
him.'

'You're kidding, right?'

'No,' she said.

'He's gorgeous, talented and creative, he's kind,
funny . . .'

'He's hardly ever funny on purpose,' Aimi interrupted. 'He says stuff that makes people laugh by accident.'

'Hey!' I said, swiping at her with a pillow. 'He's brilliant in that sketch him and Dan are doing tomorrow.'

'You so lurve him,' giggled Marybeth.

'Look at him,' I said, pointing at the picture on the screen. 'How could you not?'

'I agree with Aimi,' said Elle. 'I mean, he *is* good-looking and everything, but I could never fancy someone who was that untidy.'

'People can change,' I laughed.

'Imagine if you went out on a date with him,' said Elle, looking horrified. 'New outfit, cool movie, and he'd be so late you'd just about see the end credits by the time he got there!'

'You lost me at "imagine if you went out on a date with him",' I said, flopping backwards on to the bed and smiling up at the ceiling.

'I should've known it would be you lot making all the noise,' said Sasha, barging into the room. She

tapped her designer watch. 'Lights out. Remember what that means?'

'We don't have to look at your face any more?' I said, leaning up on my elbows.

'Maybe she glows in the dark,' muttered Aimi, and the four of us burst into fresh giggles.

'If you've finished . . .' she said. 'You, you and scholarship girl, get back to your rooms.' She pointed at Elle, Aimi and Marybeth. 'Lights off is in ten minutes. If you're not back by then, you'll have to find your way in the dark.'

She turned round, ready to do her usual stalking-off bit, and bumped straight into the senior girls' prefect, Zoe Morrison.

Zoe's cool. She's a year eleven and an amazing ballerina. Unlike Sasha, she never gets mouthy over the fact she's a prefect, and is totally fair if anyone asks her to sort stuff out around the dorms.

Seeing Sasha smack straight into her, kind of tipped the rest of us over the edge. We collapsed laughing, and it got even worse when Sasha scurried off along the corridor looking totally embarrassed.

'Another minute, girls,' said Zoe, trying not to giggle herself. 'It is nearly lights out, so you'll have to call it a day.'

'No worries,' said Aimi, and Zoe left, shutting the door behind her.

Elle stood up and straightened her jeans. 'We probably should go,' she said sensibly.

'Wait!' I said. Something had just flashed on my computer. I nudged the mouse, and saw what we'd been waiting for all evening – Jack's message.

CaptainJack: Say hello to your new king.

LuckyStar: Yeah, because that tells us everything we need to know. What happened? Was Rufus convinced?

DrummerDude: Totally.

CaptainJack: Dan interrupted us halfway through, but we couldn't stop, so we told him the story about Noah's parents too.

LuckyStar: He didn't know it was a scam?

DrummerDude: No. I have to go and message him in a minute to tell him the truth.

CaptainJack: That's how convincing we were. Dan was practically crying with sympathy for Noah.

DrummerDude: He was not!

LuckyStar: I've got a great story from last Christmas about Jack crying.

CaptainJack: Night.

'Cool,' I said, shutting the computer down. 'I wasn't sure they'd be able to pull that off.'

'Hang on,' said Elle. 'What about Rufus's sister? I

bet she's just as worried about what'll happen tomorrow as we were. Why else would she have been trying to warn us what he was up to?'

I hadn't thought about it like that before.

'We should let her know everything's OK,' I said, and the others nodded.

'SOS, remember,' said Marybeth.

I thought for a minute, then started typing.

Search Off – Solved!

'Brilliant,' said Elle.

'Sorted Out, Singer,' said Aimi.

'We're off,' said Marybeth.

Chapter Ten

I'd half been expecting it to rain on the day of the showcase, as if Rufus could have planned it in advance as part of his whole sabotage thing. But when I woke up and drew my dorm-room curtains, it was a perfect, bright, sunny Saturday morning. As I checked the web site for messages one last time and made sure my hair looked OK, there was a beeping noise from my pocket. I pulled my mobile out and flipped it open.

R U ready? Am in A's rm. She's changed 6 times since b-fast. Help me! E x

I grinned and grabbed my things.

'You look amazing,' I assured Aimi two minutes

later, as Elle and I practically dragged her away from the mirror.

It was true. She was wearing this cool retro-style dress over dark denim jeans with a pair of cute, punky Mary-Jane-style trainers, and her hair was tied back, so the blue streaks were way less noticeable.

'I'm not sure,' she groaned. 'I just don't want my parents to get all judgemental on me before they've seen us performing.'

'They won't,' I said firmly, and Elle shut the door behind us.

We headed for Marybeth's room next, a little way down the corridor.

'Look who it isn't,' sneered Sasha as she strutted past looking wildly overdressed in a pair of skin-tight jeans, designer top and strappy heels.

'Hi, Zoe,' said Aimi, looking past Sasha.

She whipped round, only to find herself staring at an empty corridor.

'*So* not funny,' she sneered, tottering off on her high heels.

'Nice *bumping* into you, Sash,' I called after her, and the three of us arrived at Marybeth's door giggling.

'Are we meeting the others outside?' she asked, as we made our way towards the stairs.

'In about fifteen –' I said, and then stopped. 'Wow!'

We'd just come round a corner and found ourselves looking at what seemed like every girl boarder in the academy. They were lined up along the windows at the front of the building, watching the main entrance as if they were waiting for Hollywood superstars to arrive instead of their parents. In Noah's case, of course, they were the same thing.

Suddenly, someone squealed, and all four of us jumped.

'It's my mum and dad!' said a tall fair-haired girl, pushing her way out of the group and dashing for the stairs. Five girls tried to squeeze into her now-empty spot.

We watched for a few minutes as more parents arrived, more people squealed, and everyone speculated on who the visitors trooping into the building might be. Students' families, children hoping to start at the academy next year, a couple of famous ex-students, newspaper reporters and, according to an overexcited year-ten student, two men wearing dark glasses who were definitely talent scouts.

'Come on,' said Elle eventually, and we made our way downstairs and out into the grounds.

Outside, there were hundreds of visitors standing around in little groups, talking and laughing and looking excited. Then, as we walked towards the amphitheatre, the groups changed. They were made up of students, some of them in costume, and all running through lines, or stretching, or warming up their voices.

'Oi,' said Jack, appearing behind us.

'Where's Noah?' asked Marybeth.

Jack pointed at two figures standing a short distance away. Noah and Dan, both in costume, ready for their comedy sketch.

'Hey!' Aimi shouted over to them.

They both turned round and spotted us.

'Nice threads,' said Marybeth, as they walked over. 'Who are you meant to be again?'

'I,' said Dan, smoothing down the smart suit he was wearing, 'am a successful businessman, about to visit a drive-thru burger joint.'

'And I –' Noah adjusted his waiter's uniform – 'am the dopey employee who misinterprets his order with hilarious consequences.'

'"Dopey employee",' said Aimi thoughtfully. 'What made you think of Noah for the part, Dan?'

Before he could answer, there was a crackling noise from the amphitheatre behind us. Ms Lang had just limped out on to the stage with her cane and her poodle, Mister Binks, and switched the microphone on.

'Aw,' said Marybeth, who has a total soft spot for Mister Binks.

'Ladies and gentlemen . . .' announced Ms Lang in her clear, crisp voice. The groups of people further away who hadn't noticed her, stopped talking immediately, and the grounds were silent. '. . . students, teachers, friends. Welcome to The Verity Lang Academy for the Performing Arts, and to our very special summer showcase.'

There was a round of applause.

'As I'm sure most of you know, this summer marks twenty years since we opened our doors to students of music and drama, teaching them alongside our existing dancers. In the years since, we have seen many wonderfully talented young people

122

come through our doors and, as a teacher, it has been a privilege to teach and nurture those talents.'

Her voice wobbled, and a tear slid down her cheek as she spoke. Adults can be such saps. Mr Walsh, the academy's ballet pianist, leaned forward and passed her a tissue. Mister Binks, who for some reason hates Mr Walsh, growled and tried to nip his ankle.

After that, I kind of zoned out a bit. Ms Lang's speeches are famously long.

'Ladies and gentlemen,' I eventually heard her say, 'it is with great pleasure and tremendous pride I invite you to enjoy the day's festivities and your visit to The Verity Lang Academy for the Performing Arts.'

'This is it!' squeaked Aimi, and even though our grand finale performance was hours away, I felt a familiar surge of pre-show nerves.

'Is it weird that I'm totally nervous for Noah?' I asked Elle as we went to find seats for his comedy sketch, just after six o'clock.

She considered for a minute. 'Yes,' she said.

'Where are the others?' I said, peering around, trying to spot Aimi, Jack and Marybeth in the crowd.

'I don't know,' said Elle. 'It's getting pretty crowded in here, though. You grab those seats and I'll go and find them.

She darted off, and I sat down at the end of a row of five empty chairs.

'Sorry,' I said to a year-seven girl and her parents who came along a few seconds later and tried to sit down. 'I'm holding these seats for someone.'

They wandered off and I looked around, hoping the others wouldn't be long. As I sat fidgeting, there was a sudden tap on my shoulder. I turned round and found myself face to face with Greg Hansen and Michelle Albright, sitting behind me.

'Hi,' said Greg, flashing his movie-star smile. 'It's Laurie, isn't it?'

'Yes,' I said, smiling back at him. For a second, I wasn't sure how he'd recognised me, but then I remembered the photos on our web site. 'You're Noah's parents.'

'It's so nice to finally meet you,' said Michelle.

'We've heard a lot about you,' said Greg, and I felt my face go red.

'We haven't seen Noah yet,' Michelle said confidentially. 'Greg thought it might make him more nervous, seeing us before the performance.'

'My mum and dad always say the same,' I said. 'My older brother too.'

'He's also in Lucky Six, right?' asked Greg.

'No.' I grimaced. 'Jack's my younger brother, and a total pain.'

They laughed, and for a few minutes, we chatted happily, like we were old friends. Seriously weird considering I was sitting there with two of the biggest movie stars on the planet.

'This must be it,' said Michelle, moving her hands up to her mouth. She was looking at the stage and I turned round to see Mrs D'Silva walking out from the wings.

'Enjoy it,' I said, turning round in my seat, just as Elle, Jack, Aimi and Marybeth slid into the row beside me.

'Was that Greg Hansen and Michelle Albright you were talking to?' hissed Aimi, as the audience applauded.

I nodded, still hardly believing it myself. As the applause died away, Noah came whistling out across the stage, dressed in his burger-boy costume. Dan had made a few changes to the script since I'd last seen them run through it, and the jokes were even funnier than before. The audience laughed loads and when the sketch finished, they applauded so hard Dan and Noah took three encores!

'That was brilliant,' said Aimi. 'Although I still think Noah was typecast.'

I grinned, then turned round to see if Greg and Michelle had enjoyed it. As we talked, the others gathered round, all eager to join in, and Noah's parents recognised them, just like they had me.

Elle looked at her watch. 'It's nearly time,' she said.

'We have to go,' I apologised to Greg and Michelle. 'We need to get changed and tune up before our performance.'

126

'Of course,' said Michelle. 'We'll see you all afterwards.'

I hesitated for a minute.

'This might sound weird,' I said to Greg and Michelle, 'but there's another performance you should try and catch.' I pointed it out in the programme. 'Rufus Donovan and Sasha Quinn-Jones. It'll be . . . unmissable,' I said. 'And I know Rufus would love a few words of wisdom afterwards, if you've got time.'

'Sure,' said Michelle. 'Thanks for the tip.'

'What, in the name of Mr Hooper's stinky old elbow patches, did you go and say that for?' asked Jack, as we hurried off to get changed.

'If they watch Rufus and Sasha, they're going to miss the start of our show,' Aimi complained.

'Only a few minutes,' I said. 'The amphitheatre stage is running late anyway.'

They didn't seem convinced.

'What's the point in holding a grudge?' I said. 'The best way to get back at Rufus is to let him know we're on to him, but we're bigger than him. No getting revenge or playing stupid tricks to pay him back.'

'Fill him with kindness,' said Elle wisely.

I giggled. '*Kill* him with kindness,' I corrected her. 'But, yeah. Something like that.'

And that was about it. With Rufus out of the picture, all our hours of rehearsing finally paid off. It was our best show ever.

'Yeah!' screamed Aimi, as the crowd roared their approval at the end of our performance.

We all moved to the front of the stage to take a bow and, as I looked out into the crowd, it seemed like the entire academy, as well as every single visitor, had been watching us. Somewhere near the front, at the side of the stage, I caught sight of Greg and Michelle and, to my amazement, Rufus was standing oblivious alongside them with his family – a stocky, balding man, a woman wearing glasses and a girl, shorter than Rufus with straighter hair, but unmistakably his twin sister. As I watched them, Rufus looked round and jumped in surprise, staring at Greg and Michelle with a shell-shocked expression on his face. The girl saw it, and laughed.

'Look!' I yelled to the others, pointing at the little group.

'Rufus's sister?' Elle shouted back over the still-applauding crowd.

'It must be.'

'You rock!' Aimi screamed at her.

'She can't hear you,' I laughed.

But as I said it, the girl looked straight at us and winked. Rufus had spotted us watching too, and his expression got lost somewhere between star-struck and ashamed and confused.

'What's she doing?' Marybeth yelled in my ear.

Rufus's sister was making her way closer to the stage.

'She can't resist me any longer,' bellowed Jack.

'She's chucking rotten fruit at you, more like,' I shouted back, as the girl pulled something out of her bag and threw it on to the stage.

I bent down to pick it up.

'A monkey?' said Aimi, as they all gathered round to look.

The stuffed toy had a gift tag tied round its neck and I turned it over to read the message.

'What does it say?' yelled Noah.

'Students Outwit Sabotage,' I read, grinning. 'Six Officially Sensational.'

Like any of us were about to argue with that.

FACT FILE   STAR SIGNS   GUIDE TO...   BEAUTY

LAURIE

NAME: Laurie Hunt
AGE: 14
STAR SIGN: Sagittarius
HAIR: Straight and auburn
EYES: Green
LOVES: Noah, writing songs, singing, acting, going to
watch her brother's band, Hype, and solving
mysteries with her friends
HATES: Being teased by Noah, seeing Sasha pick on
Marybeth and sitting around doing nothing when there
are mysteries to be solved
WORST CRINGE EVER: The time she was trying to
impress Noah with her new dance routine and didn't
realise her skirt was tucked into her knickers. Eek!

OK, SO YOU WANT TO BE A POP STAR, BUT YOU KNOW IN
YOUR HEART THAT IT'S NOT A PROPER JOB. HERE'S WHAT
YOU'RE ACTUALLY DESTINED TO DO WHEN YOU GROW UP . . .

ARIES
You like a challenge and love running about so, as a Fire
sign, a job as a fire-fighter would be great!

TAURUS
You're a real nature-lover! Taureans are big on
gardening, so tending roses all day could be the job for
you!

GEMINI
You're a natural-born salesperson and have the gift of
the gab. In fact, you're so talented you could even sell
woolly jumpers to sheep!

CANCER
You're naturally caring so you'd be good at babysitting
or working in an animal rescue centre. Or both – if you
have the time!

LEO
You like to make yourself heard and love a smart outfit.
That's why you'd do well as a really scary sergeant
major in the army!

VIRGO
Because you love paperclips, folders, computers, pens
and filing cabinets, any office job would suit you just
fine!

LIBRA
You love to know everything about the people around you, which makes you a great listener! You'd make a brilliant agony aunt!

SCORPIO
Scorpios are really clever and know pretty much everything – past, present and future. When you grow up, you're going to be a fortune teller – but you probably know that already!

SAGITTARIUS
You hate being in one place for more than 43 seconds. Any job that involves leaping from one point to another is the job for you. Maybe you should consider pole-vaulting!

CAPRICORN
Many Capricorns work in TV and film, but prefer to be researchers or producers than the star of the show as they're real behind-the-scenes types.

AQUARIUS
This is the sign of the inventor and being a mad-professor type would suit you down to the ground – as long as you don't lock yourself away on your own for too long (you're far too sociable for that!).

PISCES
You're the artist of the zodiac. Any job which involves cutting up paper, making sculptures, painting pictures and wearing strange clothes would suit you. Ever thought about being an art teacher?

BEAUTY & THE FEAST!

MAKE A TASTY FACE-TREAT USING THE CONTENTS OF
THE KITCHEN CUPBOARDS. AND IF A BIT ACCIDENTALLY
GOES IN YOUR MOUTH, GOBBLE IT UP! YUM!

COME CLEAN!

If you want to put some zing into your skin,
try this facial cleanser . . .

YOU'LL NEED

- Freshly-squeezed lemon juice
- Plain yoghurt
- A small bowl
- Cotton-wool pads
- Water
- A small towel

WHAT TO DO:

1. Mix together one tablespoon of yoghurt and one teaspoon
of lemon juice in a small bowl
2. Smooth the mixture on to clean skin with your fingertips
3. Leave for a minute or so
4. Wipe off with cotton-wool pads
5. Splash some water on your face
6. Gently pat dry with a nice fluffy towel

ET VOILA

FRUITY BEAUTY

Almost any mashed fruit can be used for this juicy face pack.
Here's how to make it . . .

YOU'LL NEED:

- 3 strawberries, or half a banana will work well
- A tablespoon of oatmeal
- A tablespoon of cream or yoghurt
- A teaspoon of honey
- A medium-sized bowl

WHAT TO DO:

1. Mash your chosen fruit
in the bowl, add the
oatmeal, cream (or yoghurt)
and honey and stir the
mixture together with a fork
2. Apply it to clean skin and then
let it work its magic
3. After ten minutes or so, rinse it all off with water
4. Eat the leftovers

DO YOU HAVE THE X-FACTOR?

WANT TO BE THE NEXT BAND ARRIVING ON PLANET POP?
HERE'S HOW TO DO IT . . .

YOU'LL NEED:
• The desire to be a star
• A bubbly personality and a wild imagination
• A love of singing and/or dancing
• Pens, paper and scissors
• A cassette player that records
• A camera/video camera (optional)
• A stack of teen magazines (for inspiration!)

Now you can set about form your very own girl band
in ten easy steps:

1. JOT DOWN WHO'S GOING TO PLAY WHICH INSTRUMENT
If you decide that you're not going to play instruments write down
what you'll be doing instead.

2. APPOINT A MANAGER
You'll need a good organiser to make it big. They'll need to make
snap decisions – especially when there are arguments!

3. CHOOSE A POP STAR NAME
Call yourself by a nickname (if you have one), a crazy title, or just
choose a name you've always liked and make it yours!

4. NAME YOUR BAND
The possibilities here are endless! A street, school, a favourite
word or even your initials can work well. But remember, your
manager always has the final say!

POP   FUN   QUIZ   GAMES

5. WRITE A COUPLE OF SONGS
This is easier said than done, so if you find it too difficult, you could just choose your two favourite songs and 'cover' them in your own unique style!

6. RECORD YOUR SONGS
If you've managed to get your hands on a tape recorder, sing until your heart's content!

7. MAKE A PROMOTIONAL VIDEO
Have any of you got access to a video camera? If so, then try making a three-minute film to go with one of your songs.

8. WORK OUT A DANCE ROUTINE
Make sure it fits with the song. Many girl bands have adopted what's known as 'literal' dancing, which means they act out the words they're singing.

9. CREATE AN IMAGE
Get your clothes, hair and attitude right and this will help to make people take you seriously. Try flicking through magazines for ideas and cut out the fashion pictures you like.

10. THINK UP A SLOGAN
What message are you trying to send out to your fans? What are your songs saying? Think up a catchy phrase that sums you up!

And there you have it – a fab new band, ready to take the world by storm. All you need now is faith in your ability - oh, and a recording contract of course!

GOOD LUCK!

FACT FILE   STAR SIGNS   GUIDE TO...   BEAUTY

 LAURIE'S GUIDE TO BROTHERS

THINK YOU'VE GOT THE BROTHER FROM HELL?
CHECK OUT THIS MINI QUIZ AND FIND OUT . . .

- Does he try to act cute in front of your friends? YES NO
- Are you always arguing with him? YES NO
- Does he always tell on you to the grown-ups? YES NO
- Would you rather not hang out with him? YES NO
- Does he make life difficult for you? YES NO
- Should he have more respect for you? YES NO
- Is he sometimes *reeeally* embarrassing? YES NO
- Do you have totally different interests and hobbies? YES NO
- Does he make fun of you in front of his mates? YES NO
- Would you rather have a sister any day? YES NO

If you answered 'yes' to two or more of the above questions,
it's likely you have yourself a beast of a bro! So, what to do?

LAURIE'S TOP TIPS:
If your brother has upset you, you need to show him. Tears can
work with older brothers and giving your little bro a good telling
off can sometimes have the desired effect. But big brothers can
see through fake tears, and little brothers will often ignore a
scolding. Why not try setting an example by saving the tears
and tantrums. Calmly talk things through instead and you just
might just get some results!

Can't wait for the next book in the series?

Here's a sneak preview of

Breaking
and
Entering

Available now from all good bookshops,

or visit: (egmont.co.uk/luckysix)

Chapter One

When you think about it, if I hadn't had the row with Aimi – the bigger than normal, pretty much enormous row – none of this might have happened. The two of us argue all the time. She's one of my best friends, and a brilliant guitarist, but she's got this thing about being the centre of attention. Mostly, our rows flare up, one of us storms off and then we're back to normal after a few hours. This time, though, Aims turned up at every rehearsal in a stinking mood. We were meant to be rehearsing for a gig Elle had booked at the shopping mall in our local town centre, and I'd written out a list of songs I thought we should play.

'Why is it always you who gets to decide, Laurie?' snapped Aimi, as I passed it round.

'Er, maybe because I was the one who spent all of last night going through our songs instead of watching lame-brain TV,' I said.

'Who even says we need a list?' she argued.

'OK,' I said, 'we'll just rehearse everything we know, then play what we feel like on the day.'

'What's wrong with that?' she shrugged.

'Duh! It would take, like, a month, and we've got less than a week till the show.'

'Don't "duh" me,' said Aimi, raising her voice.

'Duh, I think I just did.'

I know. Mature, huh? But she was seriously getting on my nerves, *and* wasting rehearsal time.

'I've had enough of this,' she said, yanking off her guitar.

'What?'

'Following orders. Being in your stupid band,' she yelled.

'Get over yourself,' I shouted back. 'That's not how it is, and you know it.'

'Yeah?' she said. 'You know what else I know? I'm leaving. Permanently.'

141

And before anyone could stop her she snatched up her guitar case and walked out, slamming the door behind her.

None of us believed it for a second – Aimi's all about playing the drama queen. For once, though, we were wrong. Three days later, we'd all tried changing her mind, but it seemed like a total lost cause.

'She *can't* leave,' said Marybeth. 'I mean, I know she can be a pain, but things wouldn't be the same without her.'

We were sitting in the common room, Marybeth, Elle, Jack, Noah and me. Sort of an emergency meeting to work out what we were going to do.

'Maybe we should set up auditions,' said Jack. 'You know, in case she definitely does leave.'

He is so sensitive.

'I thought you liked Aimi,' said Elle.

'I do,' Jack told her. 'I'm just saying.'

'Well, don't,' I snapped.

'Just because she won't listen to you,' said Jack. 'I nearly had her convinced yesterday. She was seriously thinking about changing her mind.'

I looked at him doubtfully.

'It's true,' said Marybeth. 'We both went to see her, but she didn't want to back down.'

'You heard about her parents?' said Noah.

I shook my head.

'About them cancelling their visit?' said Marybeth, and Noah nodded. 'They called at the weekend and told her they had to stay in Tokyo because they're working on this really important project.'

Something clicked into place in my brain.

'*That's* why she was in such a foul mood at the rehearsal,' I said.

'I guess,' said Marybeth. 'You know how much she'd been looking forward to seeing them.'

'I wish she'd hurry up and get over it,' said Jack. 'We're going to sound rubbish on Saturday without her.'

Elle shook her head. 'I asked her about that. She's still leaving, but she says she hasn't left yet, so she'll play on Saturday.'

'No way!' said Marybeth.

'How did you persuade her?' I asked.

'It wasn't easy,' said Elle, 'and she's not exactly thrilled about it, but I told her she'd agreed to the booking months ago, before she decided to leave, and it would be unprofessional not to be there.'

'Cunning,' said Noah admiringly.

'I told you she didn't really want to leave,' said Jack, leaning back in his chair and swinging his feet up on to the table.

But I had a feeling it would take more than a few

hours at Lowfield Shopping Centre to change Aimi's mind.

By the time Saturday morning arrived, despite what Elle had said, I was still half expecting Aimi to bail out at the last minute. So I was seriously relieved when I saw her trudging down the front steps of the academy to meet us.

'All set?' said Miss Diamond, our singing teacher and chaperone for the gig.

I nodded, and we piled into the school minibus (which doubles as our very glamorous tour bus) as she started the engine.

It felt strange, the six of us being together again, as if it had been longer than a week since my row with Aimi. Part of me had been hoping Jack was right, that playing the gig together would convince Aimi to stay, but as we arrived and set up in a strained kind of silence, it began to seem less and less likely.

'Hey,' said Noah, peering out over the makeshift

stage into the gathering crowd, 'who d'you reckon that guy is?'

I followed the direction of his gaze and saw a short, balding man wearing a badly fitting pinstripe suit, purple braces and a cowboy hat.

'No idea,' I said. 'Maybe he's finally woken up to the fact his wardrobe is a disaster and he's here for the shopping.'

Noah grinned.

'Looks like a talent scout to me,' said Elle, coming up behind us.

'You think?' I said.

'Yep. You can tell by the outfit.'

I checked my watch. 'Five minutes,' I said. 'I guess we'd better hurry up if we want to impress him.'

Considering the weird atmosphere in the minibus, and the fact we hadn't rehearsed with Aimi in over a week, the gig went pretty well. The small crowd who'd gathered at the start had grown to more or less fill the mall by the time we finished.

'Thank you, Lowfield, and goodnight!' shouted Jack into my microphone as we made our way offstage.

'Cut the cheese, Wart-face,' I hissed, dragging him away. 'There's a talent scout in the audience and I don't want him thinking we're all losers.'

I scrambled down off the back of the stage, following the others, and ducked into the curtained backstage area.

'A talent scout?' said Jack, catching up with me a minute later. 'Where?'

I pulled a bottle of water out of my bag and took a swig.

'I don't know,' I said. 'Somewhere out in the crowd.'

'Try over there,' said Elle, pointing through a gap in the back of the curtains. 'He grabbed Aimi the second she stepped offstage.'

'Why would he only want to talk to her?'

'Maybe she's telling him about all of us. You know, kind of as a representative of the band,' said Noah.

'The band she's about to leave,' said Elle doubtfully.

'He looks a bit dodgy to me,' said Jack.

He had a point.

'I think we should go over there,' I said decisively. 'She's not exactly safe, hanging about talking to a total stranger.'

Elle nodded. 'Come on,' she said, and we made our way across to Aimi and the talent scout.

'Nice to meet you, ladies,' he said, once we'd introduced ourselves. Aimi scowled. 'Rich Saunders,' the talent scout added, fishing two business cards out of his pocket and handing one to each of us. Elle looked down at hers and frowned.

'That was quite a performance back there,' he said. 'Not a bad little band you've got going.'

'Thanks,' I said uncertainly.

'This little lady's your star, of course,' he continued. 'Very talented guitarist. I was just telling her how keen I am to hear more of her stuff. Solo material, that is,' he added, just in case we got the wrong end of the stick.

'Really?' I said, looking straight at Aimi and raising my eyebrows.

'Really,' she said, and to prove her point she pulled a CD out of her bag and handed it to Mr Saunders.

'It's got all my solo stuff on it.' She pointed to the track listing, just beneath her name, a photo of herself and our web address. 'Like I was saying, I don't just play guitar. I write songs, and sing too. I've never really had the chance to do either in the band,' she said pointedly. 'That's why I want to go solo.'

'Lovely,' said Mr Saunders, dropping the CD into his pocket. 'I'll have a listen, and you give me a call in a few days, when you've had time to think things over. You've got my card.'

He reached out and shook her hand, then walked off into the crowd of shoppers.

Elle and I took all of two seconds to drag Aimi backstage again.

'What on earth was that about?' I hissed.

Aimi laughed. 'Someone's finally recognised I'm more talented than you are. Get over it.'

'I don't even think he's a real talent scout,' said Elle, who's way better at ignoring Aimi's insults than I am. 'His record company,' she said, flapping the business card under Aimi's nose, 'I've never heard of them.'

'What, and you know *all* the record companies?' snapped Aimi. 'You just can't handle the fact he wants me and not you.'

And before either of us had a chance to argue she stalked off towards the exit.

If things in the minibus had been uncomfortable on the way to the gig, they were a million times worse as we drove back to school.

'Is anything wrong?' asked Miss Diamond.

You'd pretty much have had to be a lump of rock with no eyes, no ears and no brains, not to realise something was going on.

'*I'm* fine,' said Aimi. 'I just out-performed everyone today and some people can't handle it.'

Miss Diamond didn't seem to know what to say and, not daring to start another argument in front of her, the minibus fell into miserable silence again.

I sat there, wondering for the millionth time that week what it would be like playing without Aimi. It wasn't as if the band would fall apart without her – when our bass player left last year, splitting up didn't occur to any of us – but we wouldn't find another guitarist at the academy as good. Maybe there were more important things than being the best, though. Things like chilling out instead of flying off the handle all the time. I glanced over at Aimi again. She glared back at me and, however hard I tried to stop it, one thought kept creeping into my head – would it be such a bad thing if she did leave?